LOVE IN THE LIGHTS

CHRISTMAS AT THE RANCH

BRITNEY M. MILLS

CRYSTAL CANYON PUBLISHING

Copyright © 2019 by Britney M Mills

Cover design by Blue Water Books

All rights reserved.

No part of this book may be reproduced in any form or by any electronic or mechanical means, including information storage and retrieval systems, without written permission from the author, except for the use of brief quotations in a book review.

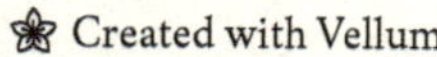 Created with Vellum

$\mathcal{N}$atalie Lynch stuffed her container of salad and dressing into her insulated lunch bag, checking the time on the oven. 7:15 a.m. Breathing a sigh of relief, she was thankful she just might make it to work early today. It was the middle of October, and she'd already received a warning from the principal.

"Dad! Come take your pills!" she called down the hall. When she heard nothing, she stormed to the closed bedroom door two doors down the hallway. After knocking once, she turned the knob, trying to adjust her eyes to the dim light inside. She found the lump on the bed and walked over to it, poking a few times. "Dad. You need to get up. Your pills are on the counter, and I put some eggs in the oven."

A groan came from the mound of blankets, and he finally rolled over. "What time is it?" His voice sounded like a rusty saw.

"Well after seven. I've got to get going, or I'll be late for school. The horses are all fed and brushed. Starlight needs to be walked today, though. Can you get that done before I get home?" Natalie stared at him, arm on her hip, trying to look serious.

Her father waved her off. "I'll get to it. Just let a man sleep. You've been pestering me since you moved in."

"My teaching salary can only go so far toward the bills, Dad. We need you to get back to working with your horses. There's only so much I can do with your marketing if you don't have horses ready to sell." She could feel the bite coming through, the frustration of weeks of pushing and pulling settling over her from trying to get her stubborn father back on his feet.

"Way to go straight for the heart, Natalie," he said, throwing back the covers. He lowered his feet to the ground, the large leg cast making a thud against the floor. He rubbed at his eyes and reached for the crutches Natalie held out for him. "Shouldn't you be going?"

Natalie waited until he'd regained his balance and nodded. "Remember, no drinking with these pills. I've set a reminder on your phone to take the next dose at one this afternoon. I'll be home—"

"I know, I know," he said, cutting her off. "Get going before you're the first teacher to get a tardy." He grinned at that, and Natalie rolled her eyes. At least he wasn't all vinegar this morning.

She grabbed her jacket, purse, and lunch box on the way out, almost forgetting her keys on the wall. With a wave, she moved out to her Honda and was grateful when it started up on the first try. She'd have to get up earlier once the weather turned colder. Her late 90s car wasn't going to start easily once the ice formed.

Pulling onto the curving road down the small canyon from her home, she glanced at the clock. 7:28 a.m. Stepping on the accelerator, she just hoped the principal wouldn't be arriving at the same time. She didn't need another lecture about being late.

Going through her morning checklist, she was able to mentally cross off several items, helping her feel like today wasn't a complete waste of time. The stables were finally looking somewhat decent after her daily cleaning, and the horses didn't take forever to brush anymore. But she'd have to do more work with social media for her father's horse training business. They needed more horses to train, and she hoped that by showing him the business was growing, he'd snap out of his funk and get back to how she remembered him when she was eleven, before her mom divorced him and moved them to her hometown in Utah.

"One thing at a time, Nat," she said out loud. She wouldn't be able to change everything in a day, or even a few weeks. A little at a time was all she could ask of herself.

It was time to teach high school English, something she loved more than she'd thought after writing all those long, boring papers in college. It was the one thing that had pulled her through her own divorce nearly five years ago, following her six-month marriage to Craig Morgan. Changing the lives of students, helping them see how great learning could be, was what she lived for now and what would carry her through to the next part of her life.

There wasn't a lot of room for extra stuff in her life at the moment, and dating was the last thing she could expect from a small town like Coldwater Creek. But a girl could fantasize about dressing up and dancing with a handsome man.

She shook her head and kept driving. Now was not the time to start worrying about love. With teaching, including being the student council advisor and the teacher over the school plays and musicals, and then her father's horses on top, she had plenty to keep her occupied until she was old and gray.

CHAPTER 2

*E*aston McBride walked in through the back door of the old ranch house, placing his cowboy hat on the hook and taking off his coat. Once he'd removed his shoes as well, he walked into the kitchen, breathing in deeply as the smell of eggs, bacon, and pancakes wafted to his nose.

"Smells good, Mom," he said, sliding onto one of the barstools next to the island.

"It's about time you all got done. I was worried the food would be cold." His mother moved around the kitchen, pulling plates from the cupboard and dishing out the food in the frying pans. Grabbing some toast and adding it to his plate, she slid it in front of him. "Where's your father and the twins?"

Easton focused on buttering his toast. "I'm not sure. Dad is fiddling with the tractor again, and the twins disappeared over an hour ago. They didn't make it in here?" When his mother shook her head, it wasn't the biggest surprise ever. His twin brothers were known for disappearing when work was going on, and there wasn't a whole lot Easton could do about it.

"What are we going to do with them?" his mother said to no one in particular.

"They're probably out practicing for this weekend. You know how much they want to beat the Stocktons."

His mother paused, leaning on the countertop and nodded. "I can understand that, but work at the ranch pays for them to team rope. I just wish they wouldn't get so competitive."

"It was bound to happen, Mom," Easton said, laughing. He thought about the competitive streak that came from both their mother and father, and while a few of the six McBride children were somewhat laid-back, the rest weren't the best at taking defeat.

A few moments passed in silence, and Easton ate his food, loving the chewiness of the bacon his mother had cooked. She knew each one of her children's likes and dislikes as though it had been written in a book for her, and he was lucky to have her.

"I saw Celia Ashburn in town yesterday. She was asking about you again." His mother got that conspiratorial tone to her voice, making Easton groan.

"Well, tell her I'm unavailable. I'm not going on another date with her, no matter how bad you feel for her."

"Easton, you're thirty-two years old. There are only a small handful of girls around your age who are single. You might as well find someone to have by your side when you have to take over the ranch."

Nothing like making him feel better about his bachelorhood. Sure, he was over thirty and still lived at home, but being the oldest, he was set to take over the ranch.

It hadn't always been that way. He'd gotten away for college and even played a few games with the New England Patriots before he'd broken his leg so bad that even several surgeries hadn't been able to put it right, leaving him with a deep limp. With the weather changing, the ache kept him up at night, compounding the exhaustion he felt from ranch life.

"I love you, Mom, but just let me figure out my love life, okay? You've got other sons you can pester about finding a girlfriend as well. I'm sure Walker could use a good push by now." He glanced up and found himself facing the most intense glare he'd ever seen.

"Walker's been the closest one to a long-term relationship, and right now, I don't want to bother him about all that. Once the lodge is finished and running, I'll make sure he feels the nudge. This lady would like some grandkids at some point. It's like once you left the NFL, you gave up on love."

Easton groaned. It was nearly eight in the morning, and he'd already put three hours into his workday. This was not a debate he wanted to open up this early. Taking his last piece of bacon, he stood up and chewed on it as he walked over and rinsed off his plate.

He turned and kissed his mother's cheek. "It'll work out, Mom. Just let me worry about it for now." With quick steps, he moved back to the mudroom, replacing his coat and hat. He still had plenty to get done before showing up to coach football practice at the high school. And the last thing he wanted to do was think about dating any of the women in Coldwater Creek.

CHAPTER 3

The bell rang to signal the end of third period, meaning the students and teachers were all heading to lunch.

"Okay, class. That's it for today. Make sure to put your essays into the box and have a great day." Natalie moved over to her desk, shuffling together several of the papers she'd used for the lesson and breathing out a sigh of relief once everything was in order.

"Um, Miss Lynch?" A young man's voice caused her to look up, and she recognized Talon Erickson, the star quarterback for the football team.

"What is it, Talon?" she asked, standing up straight. Even at her tallest, she was still several inches shorter than the tall junior.

He shifted from one leg to the other, one hand in his pocket and the other twirling a pencil. "I, uh, didn't get a chance to print out my essay because we ran out of ink at home. I wrote it in pen and did my best to make it legible. Will you accept that?" He pulled a small stack of papers out of his backpack, showing her the essay.

To her surprise, it was very neatly written and looked like it could have been typed with block lettering. She looked up at him, trying to decide what to do. Past football players had soured her opinion about current ones, but she was trying to be neutral.

"You know I said it was supposed to be typed. Is there a way you can type it up in the library during lunch?"

Talon frowned, his eyes pleading. "Will you still give me full credit for it if I turn it in by the end of the day?" The look on his face showed how much this really meant to him. And right now, with a missing essay, he'd be suspended from football until he could get his grades back up. She could already hear the fight ensuing when she benched the team's best player.

"If you get it to me within fifteen minutes of the last bell, I'll count it as on time. Next time, just make sure you come in early to type it, okay?" She raised her eyebrows and did her best to give him a stern expression. Was it really that he was out of ink? Or was this some ploy because he was an athlete?

It wasn't like this was her first teaching assignment, but he had been coming into class each day looking as though he hadn't slept well. She'd have to ask her teaching friend if there was anything going on at home. Melody seemed to know all the gossip about what was going on with the students at Coldwater Creek, and asking her was a safe zone.

She'd spent a few years teaching in a small town in northern Utah before relocating to Coldwater Creek High at the beginning of the school year, and she'd dealt with plenty of privileged athletes in that time. But she was grateful Talon wasn't one of those, or at least he hadn't ever tried to get out of assignments because of his status on the football field.

"I will. I promise. Thank you so much, Miss Lynch." He gave her a quick smile before disappearing into the crowded hall.

As much as she'd grown to detest football, she could understand it around here. Scholarships were a way out of this small town, and it didn't always matter how much talent the kids had as long as they had the grades to go with it.

She pulled her lunch bag from the bottom drawer of her desk and made her way down to the teachers' lounge. As was her usual, she'd arrived as the last bell rang and hadn't been able to put it into the fridge in the lounge. Hopefully, her salad wasn't wilted from sitting in her desk drawer all morning.

As she entered the room, it was buzzing with the three microwaves warming up various lunch options and several teachers chatting about their day or a test they'd given.

"How'd everything go today?" Melody Archer asked her, leaning over the couch where Natalie had settled. Melody was the physics teacher but had taken Natalie under her wing the first week of school.

"Not too bad. The kids were really insightful today. I love it when things like that happen." Natalie grinned, thinking over the discussion they'd had on Edgar Allen Poe in the last class.

Melody pulled a container of what looked like tomato soup out of a microwave and brought it back over to sit next to Natalie, who pulled out her salad and dumped the dressing on top. After moving the pieces back and forth to spread the dressing out more evenly, she stabbed her fork in it, reminding her of memories she'd dug up about football players.

"Well, at least one of us is having a good day. My kids decided to play a prank that ended up with several of my brand-new beakers exploding. Glass went everywhere. Janitor Todd was not thrilled." She chuckled as if she'd been in on the joke herself. "That means I'll be replacing them myself or trying to rework a whole unit next month."

"But did you enjoy said prank?" Natalie asked with a grin. The older woman seemed to relish mischief, and there was a certain twinkle in her eye about the whole thing.

Melody leaned over and whispered, "I was quite impressed, to say the least. But no one knows that, got it?" She pointed her finger at Natalie, and it was as if time had reversed within seconds, sending her back to her own high school experience.

"Got it." Natalie chuckled and took another bite of lunch. After swallowing, she turned to Melody. "Do you know if there's anything happening at the Erickson home? Talon said they'd run out of ink, so he handwrote his essay."

Melody gave her a somber expression and leaned in a bit, lowering her voice. "The father has a rare form of cancer and can't work right now. I know the mom does everything she can, but with two in high school and then three kids below that, I think money is tight."

Natalie frowned, feeling like she'd just been punched in the gut. Of course, she had to be strict with a kid who was actually struggling.

"Now I feel awful. I told him to type it up in the library during lunch."

"Well, that's what it's there for. The Ericksons are good kids. I just hope they can make it through this obstacle. The kids have been taking odd jobs to help out their mother with the payments of rent and medical bills. I heard that Principal Jackson is planning on using the Christmas Ball as a fundraiser for their family."

"That's a great idea." Sighing, Natalie stuffed another bite of salad into her mouth. Nothing worse than feeling like a heel.

The door opened, and as if he knew he was being talked about, in walked Principal Jackson, scanning the room until his eyes fell on Natalie. He took a few steps to stand before her. "Ms. Lynch, I just got word from Silver Brook Lodge that they have reserved December fifteenth as the night for the Christmas Ball. Has your council started planning for it?"

Natalie's eyes widened. "Not yet, sir. The Harvest Dance is this coming Saturday, and we're doing a few last-minute preparations for that in fourth period today. We'll get working on the Christmas Ball after that." She paused a moment and then said, "Wait, didn't the lodge burn down a long time ago?"

Principal Jackson studied her for a moment. "I'm surprised a newbie like yourself would know about that. It did burn down almost twenty years ago, but it's being rebuilt right now." He smiled like delivering this news was something he'd been waiting a long time for. "I have some help to make sure everything goes well for Christmas. I'll let him know to meet with you next week during fourth period." And as abruptly as he'd walked in, Principal Jackson turned and left the room, leaving Natalie with several questions.

Leaning over to Melody, Natalie asked, "Why the urgency with the Christmas Ball? He just said we already have a venue, which is usually half the battle in planning school dances."

A sly smile spread over her face, and Melody rolled her lips in as if ready to keep a secret. "He's been dating Dottie Perkins, and that woman loves to dress up. So just be prepared for him to be breathing down your neck to get it right."

"But the dance is nearly two months away. Why would he be planning that early?" Natalie tried to figure it out, but with every guy she'd either known or dated, they hadn't ever thought that far in advance. She'd thought Craig was different, but after three years together and then finally convincing him to marry her, she knew comfortable and easy was all he thought about. Maybe Principal Jackson could prove her theory wrong.

Melody shrugged and smiled, dunking a cracker in the last of her tomato soup.

Natalie thought about the conversation all the way up the stairs to her classroom. She was so lost in her thoughts that she didn't see a man turning the corner. Her shoulder hit his chest and sent her flying back a few steps.

Blinking a few times, she looked up and couldn't hold back a smile at the handsome man before her. "I'm so sorry. I was lost in thought."

He put up his hands and nodded with a smile. "No worries." He kept moving past her and walked down the stairs, looking back once. She noticed he walked with a limp but her attention then moved back to his attractive face.

Feeling her cheeks turn to fire, Natalie moved out of view of the staircase and back down the hall where several students milled around lockers, getting ready for the fourth and final block period of the day.

She sat at her desk, trying to concentrate on what they still needed to discuss in her student council class for this weekend, but for some reason, she couldn't get the face of the guy in the hallway out of her mind. A strong jaw, dark brown hair, and brown eyes that reminded her of a chocolate fountain. A strange sensation zipped through her at the thought of him. It had been some time since she'd been attracted to a guy, but he was definitely worth looking twice at. And his deep voice? She could get lost thinking—

"Are you all right, Ms. Lynch?" Amy Gardner asked. She was the student body president and one of Natalie's favorite people.

Looking up, Natalie forced a smile. "Um, yes. I'm just trying to remember what we need to discuss today."

Amy set a paper down in front of her and smiled. "I have

a list of things I thought we could cover. Did you have any to add?"

Natalie perused the paper and grinned. "Looks like you hit on everything I needed to talk about. Why don't you lead out once the bell rings?"

As Natalie thought about the man in the hall once more, she shook her head, knowing that with her luck, he was probably already taken in a small town like this. Best to stick with what she knew best, and that was teaching.

CHAPTER 4

*E*aston turned when he made it to the landing, looking back up at the woman with the long blonde hair one more time before remembering he'd just been called to the office by the principal. Not that that was much different from his own time attending this school, but there was something that intrigued him about the woman. Maybe it was the fact he'd never seen her before, or even her stunned reaction to running into him.

As beautiful as she was, his track record with women was next to horrible on the all-time scale. Best to find out what Principal Jackson wanted him for and leave her alone.

Opening the door to the office, he winked and grinned at Shirley, the secretary. "I take it he's in his office?"

Shirley turned, her bouffant-style hair not moving with the quickness of her action. "He's waiting for you. Let me know how it goes." The older woman grinned, and Easton chuckled as he walked a few doors back to the principal's office. She was known for being a know-it-all around town, and any little tidbit could be spread like a wildfire with her connections.

As Easton knocked twice on the open door before walking in, Principal Jackson's focus moved from his computer screen to Easton. "That was fast. I didn't think they'd find you in the building at this time of day, but Shirley assured me she'd seen you pass earlier."

Easton grinned and shook his head. "That woman must have spies all over the school."

"I wouldn't be surprised," Principal Jackson said, sitting back and intertwining his hands on the desk in front of him. "I have an assignment I need you to accept."

Easton paused, curious as to what this man in his forties could need from him. "What is it, sir?"

"I need you to help with the preparations for the Christmas Ball."

Knowing he wasn't the best with dates, Easton tried to remember what day it was. "But that isn't for two more months. Isn't there another dance coming up this weekend?"

The man on the other side of the desk leaned forward, his hands raised as if trying to reassure Easton. "Well, this year we've decided to donate the proceeds of the ball to the Erickson family as part of their Christmas. With the father undergoing treatment for lung cancer, they could use quite a bit of help. We won't be disclosing who the money will go to, just that it will be a Sub-for-Santa opportunity."

That was definitely a good cause. He'd seen the Erickson boys in what looked to be dirty and tattered clothing in the locker room after practices and games. He'd tried to talk to them about their home life, but some kids just didn't open up as easily as others. Even ones with talent like theirs.

"What is it you want me to do?" Easton asked, still not connecting all the dots as to why he was being asked to help.

"Since you're their coach, I thought it might be nice if you helped out with the marketing of it all. Besides, your brother has agreed to let us use the event room at Silver Brook Lodge once it's done."

That was news to him. He and Walker were really close, but he hadn't heard that the school wanted to use the new lodge reception hall for the dance. "Are you sure it will be done in time?"

After retiring from the rodeo at the end of last year, his brother had bought the old hotel and had been working for the last six months to rebuild the lodge that had burned down years ago. They were making good progress, but to have it ready for an event like this, Easton wasn't sure it would be done.

"He assured me it would be. So, if you need to coax him or help him along to get it done, I would appreciate it."

From the look on the man's face, Easton could tell there was something more. "Is there something else riding on this ball other than that? What about Dorothy Perkins? You two are dating, and from what my mom said, it's getting pretty serious." He gave the older man a mischievous grin, enjoying the principal's discomfort as he squirmed and readjusted his tie.

"We're dating, but I'm not to that point yet. The student council will be meeting during fourth period on Monday to discuss plans for the Christmas Ball. It would be nice if you could make it."

That meant another extra-early start to the day. His usual wake-up time was five in the morning in order to get all the chores done around the ranch so his father wouldn't be worried about them until Easton returned from football practices and games later in the evening. He was already burning the light at both ends, but if it would help out the family of two of his athletes, he'd be willing to sacrifice more.

"I'll do what I can to make it to the meeting, sir."

Both men stood, and Principal Jackson reached across his

desk to shake Easton's hand. "I appreciate it, Easton. I know it's a lot to ask, but you know I trust you with big things like this. And with how you've turned our football program around in the last five years, well, I just want to say thank you. We've had the highest record of football players graduate, some even with honors, and go on to college under your tenure than probably all of the history of this school. Keep up the good work."

Heat warmed the tops of Easton's ears, and he ducked his head and turned to leave. "No problem, Steve. It's the least I can do to give back after all the opportunities I was given."

He walked out the door before he could see the look of pity everyone displayed the moment his prior career was mentioned. Sure, it had been a blow to be told after week four of his rookie season that the amount of damage from one hit couldn't be repaired enough to play again. But injury was always a possibility when playing a sport.

With the halls empty for the last period of the day, Easton walked in the direction of the locker room, knowing he needed to get practice mapped out to prepare his team for the in-state rivals they would face the next night.

He'd have to figure out a way to tell his father that one more thing had been added to his plate. Not ready to dwell on that conversation, Easton turned on the video of the team they would be playing, making sure to study for any weaknesses he'd missed in the previous four viewings.

Instead, the picture of the blonde in the hallway crept into his mind, and he wondered who she was. Definitely not one of the teachers who'd been teaching at Coldwater Creek High for several decades. He'd have to find out more about her, if only to quell the curiosity nagging in his brain.

CHAPTER 5

$\mathcal{N}$atalie made it out of the school later than usual on Friday afternoon to find that the parking lot was less crowded than when she'd arrived that morning. Sitting in her car, she turned the ignition but heard nothing but a click. She closed her eyes, hoping it would start up with another turn of the key. The same sound came through.

How would she pay for it to go to the repair shop? And how would she get to work without a vehicle?

She dropped her head onto the steering wheel, only to jerk back when the horn sounded.

"Do you need some help?" A deep voice to her side caused her to jump. It wasn't entirely clear as the window was still shut, but as she turned, she had to remind herself to close her mouth. It was the guy she'd seen the day before, the one she'd bumped into in the hall.

She rolled down the window and tried to paste a smile on her face. "I should be fine. My car is just old and struggles sometimes."

The guy looked like he'd stepped out of a magazine, and Natalie caught herself staring at him as he glanced down at the watch on his wrist. "I have about fifteen minutes until I have to be in the locker room. Pop the hood, and I'll take a look."

Natalie bit her tongue. Had he not just heard her say she didn't need help? "Really, I've got this."

"I promise I'm not here to sabotage your car," the guy said with a sly grin. "My truck is pretty old, and I have to do a lot to get it running sometimes. This cooler weather might be causing the problem."

The way he spoke made her forget her irritation, and she popped the hood. As he lifted it up, she tried not to notice the defined muscles in his arms as he moved.

After several moments of silence, he said, "Okay, turn the key."

The same clicking sound happened, and her stomach sank. Most of her paycheck was already going toward past-due bills. She couldn't afford repairs on her car.

"Your battery looks like it might be the culprit. Let me get my truck, and we'll try to jump it." He took off, jogging over to the far corner of the parking lot. She *may* have watched his graceful movements all the way there, enjoying the look of his backside.

Shaking her head, she looked at the steering wheel. Just because he was attractive and very helpful didn't mean she needed to keep looking. She'd learned that lesson often enough that she thought she'd have immunized herself against the charms of handsome men by now.

A loud engine pulled up and around, parking in the space right next to her. The smell of the exhaust seeped into her car through the partially open window, and she coughed. He hopped out of the cab and propped up his own hood, attaching the familiar black and red cables between the two vehicles.

"Okay, turn it over."

She did as he asked, but nothing happened.

"Wait a minute, and we'll try again." With the loud noise coming from his probably 1980s truck, he moved over to her window, bringing with him a stronger smell of exhaust and something she couldn't quite pinpoint.

"Football coach, huh?" she asked, pointing to his shirt. He wore a white polo with the Coldwater Creek logo and the word *football* embroidered below it.

He shrugged, stuffing his hands into his pants pockets. "I try to help out here and there. I don't believe we've met before. I'm Easton McBride." He stuck his hand out and through her window.

The shock of the name echoed in her brain, and she mechanically shook his hand. Easton McBride, the name of the man her father had been complaining about for the past three years. He was the man who'd fired her father from his position as the defensive coach, her unknown enemy. But she'd always pictured him as some sour forty-year-old, not an attractive kind guy around thirty.

"Natalie Lynch. I'm the new English teacher here." She pointed at the school as if that needed emphasis. Her name didn't seem to ring a bell with him, and why would it? She'd never gone through the trouble of having it changed back to her maiden name of Hirsch.

He didn't seem to recognize her face either, but she'd been a shy girl when she lived in Coldwater Creek before. She remembered Easton's younger brother being in her grade, but that was the extent she could remember from so long ago. And that was ages before the football fight a few years ago, the one she hadn't been there for but had been given enough details about to last her a lifetime.

He nodded. "It's nice to meet you. I hope you're settling into Coldwater Creek."

"Yes, just fine, thank you. Should we try again?" She pointed to the engine.

"Yeah, turn it over again."

The car finally roared to life, and Natalie wasn't sure if she should be grateful or if she preferred talking to him a bit more.

As he worked to disconnect their vehicles, she leaned out the window. "Thank you for helping me out of here. I really appreciate it. Good luck with your game tonight." She turned to shift into reverse and startled when she found him leaning on her window.

"You might look into getting a new battery. I think that will solve the problem for the most part. And you should come to the game if you get the chance. I could introduce you to some more people around town after." He grinned at her, and as much as she wanted to shout no and take off out of the parking lot, she felt some part of her unable to.

Biting the corner of her mouth, she said, "I'll see what I have going on. I have a job after school, and it sometimes takes much longer than I want it to."

She saw the slight disappointment in his face before he smiled again, stood, and waved to her. Her heart beat wildly, and she did her best to calm down, knowing a guy like him could never end up with a girl like her. She was wholly broken from her last relationship, and the chances of her father having a heart attack if he found out they were dating were much higher than she wanted them to be at the moment.

Dating? She'd met the guy ten minutes ago, and he'd asked her to come watch him coach the football team. It wasn't like he'd invited her to some intimate restaurant. But he *had* mentioned making an effort to see her afterward. Maybe that was something.

Brushing it off, she focused on the list of tasks she needed to accomplish this weekend. Hopefully, she could take her mind off the handsome car starter and focus on how to get her father's business back on track.

CHAPTER 6

*E*aston watched as the new English teacher pulled away and out of the parking lot. He'd heard some of his players mention a new teacher who'd moved here from northern Utah, but he hadn't given it much thought. The only people crazy enough to accept a job up here were older, more established teachers, or ones who'd moved here with their spouses. The fact that Natalie Lynch was both young and beautiful had done something to his chest, loosening something inside.

Walking over to the football field, he saw the field crew putting on the finishing touches, painting lines and getting everything together for the game. As much as he loved real grass, with the way the Wyoming weather blew in, he wished the principal would listen to him and put in field turf. It would make for fewer dips and holes after some of the rainy and cold nights his kids had to play under.

But his thoughts went back to Natalie, causing him to wonder what had brought her to a small town like this. He'd noticed she didn't have a ring on, which was something he didn't usually worry about when helping other people around town. But after her crystal-blue eyes looked up at him with annoyance and then trust, he found he couldn't get rid of the image.

For the first time in his life, he hoped a woman would actually show up to the game, that he'd somehow manage to find her after and they could go to the diner or one of the ice cream shops that stayed open later on game nights. He'd always been the hotshot quarterback in high school but was never good at having a relationship. Probably because life on the ranch could be that demanding, much like his life now.

"Are you doing okay, Coach?" a voice asked behind him. Easton turned to find one of the Erickson boys, his eyebrows raised.

"I'm fine. What's wrong, Johnny? Why are you out here so early? Shouldn't you be getting dressed to come out with the rest of the team?" Easton searched the boy's face, trying to guess what was wrong before the truth of it hit him.

Johnny blew out a breath. "I, uh, well, my mother got the flu last night, and she can't go into work at the grocery store. I'm going to have to cover for her or she'll lose her job, which means I have to miss tonight's game." He looked down, but Easton didn't miss the disappointment written all over his face.

Easton rested one hand on the boy's shoulder. "Are things getting worse with your father?"

Johnny shrugged, swiping his hand under his nose without looking up. He moved his foot back and forth, playing with a small pebble on the sidewalk. "He's about the same, but bills are piling up. I'm really sorry, Coach."

"You're fine, Johnny. I know how much you love football, but sometimes we have to set that aside and do what's most important in the moment." He pulled the boy close, giving him a hug for a few seconds before pulling back. He reached into his pocket and pulled out his wallet. "Here's twenty bucks. Make sure to get yourself some dinner before you head in for your shift."

Johnny looked at the money as if it might turn into some poisonous reptile. Easton eased it into his hand and closed the boy's fingers around it.

With his eyes clouded with tears, Johnny looked up and nodded. "Thank you, Coach. I appreciate it. Talon is still playing tonight, so at least you'll have one of the Erickson brothers." He tried to laugh and smile, but it sounded more like a wheeze than anything.

"Good luck, son. Let me know if there's another way I can help you out." Easton watched as the boy turned and jogged back out of the gates surrounding the small field. There had been times when Easton had wondered why his life was so hard, why his dreams didn't pan out. But then there were moments like this, when he knew it had all led up to where he needed to be, and right then, he felt grateful for the health of his family and the chance he had to be both rancher and football coach.

But for one split second, a deep ache punctured his chest. He thought about Natalie, and thoughts of her led him to the conversation he'd had with his mother. Maybe his love life wasn't lost for good. He just needed to find Natalie again and ask her out properly. He'd be watching for her tonight. It was worth a shot, and maybe if Celia Ashburn saw them out together, she'd stop calling him. The potential for a double-win was there, and he smiled at the thought.

CHAPTER 7

The weekend had passed like lightning, and that was just how Natalie liked it. Since she'd moved in with her father, weekends had been the worst, usually trying to pry him out of the two bars the valley had or making sure he didn't wander off to some unknown part of the forest around their home. And with the large cast on, she found it even more difficult to control him.

Two and a half months before, she'd gotten a call that her father was in the hospital, and although they'd had limited contact throughout the years, she made the drive from Logan to Coldwater Creek to check on him. He'd been in a head-on collision with a large deer that had made its way onto the curvy canyon road that led to the Hirsch home.

After some routine testing while in the hospital for his leg, the doctor said that if her father didn't stop drinking soon, he'd be needing a new liver. Their diagnosis had helped spur her to apply for the job at the local high school. That and needing a fresh start somewhere away from where she'd grown up during her teen years, since all the memories were now soured by her grandmother's death.

She'd thought about going to the football game, just to see Easton again, but there was so much to get done around their small homestead that she couldn't really take a break. Between dragging her father out like he was a three-year-old throwing a tantrum in the supermarket just to get him to work with the horses and then making sure to answer emails and update all the social media posts, she was usually too tired to form complete sentences by seven in the evening.

Maybe it was because she hadn't been back to the house in Wyoming in over a decade, but the way she remembered it from her childhood went way beyond what it looked like now. Her father had once been the top horse trainer in Wyoming. Seeing him sink to this made her stomach tighten, knowing there had to be a lot of different aspects besides just the divorce from her mother that had caused the downfall. She'd come for a week every summer, but that didn't let her into all the problems and demons her father faced.

Her father's intake of alcohol had even been much less than usual in the past two days, and Natalie hadn't dared to ask about the difference, worried it would remind him he hadn't had a drink in a while and he'd head out to get one.

She'd made some herbal tea and brought it out to the back porch to sit in a rocker, admiring the pine trees that clumped along the mountains several hundred yards from their home. A few minutes later, her father stumbled out and sat in the other rocking chair, staring into the growing darkness surrounding them.

"Work again tomorrow?" he asked in his gruff voice.

Natalie rocked back and forth slowly and said, "Yes, no school holidays for a while. I'm just glad to have that dance last night over with." She smiled until she remembered Principal Jackson wanted her working on the Christmas Ball the next day. No rest for this girl, apparently.

"Are you sure you haven't seen the newspaper from

yesterday? I wanted to check out the news in the valley," he said, his hands folded on his lap as he rocked at a faster pace than she did.

Natalie knew where it was, but she'd made sure to hide it deep in the trash can, even pouring water over the sports section to make sure the colors bled together. Maybe that was the reason her father hadn't gotten so drunk this weekend. He hadn't been able to fume and vent over the Coldwater Creek football team.

"I saw today's paper on the doorstep. Did you read that one?"

He gave a curt nod. "Yeah, but it didn't have anything—"

"About the football team in it?" Natalie asked, straightening up a bit. It was a move she was surprised she'd played, but if her father couldn't get over the past, he'd never be able to move on.

His hard expression caused an icy feeling to travel down her spine. "So what if I want to know what's happening with my old team? Coldwater Creek had the best defensive line for years when I was coaching there. If it wasn't for that idiot McBride, I'd still be doing what I love, getting those kids scholarships just like I always did."

"Dad, it's been three years. You need to move on, find something else you're passionate about. Get back to training champion horses and winning every award there is for it. Or what about that woodworking shop you started out there in the shed? You have such a talent for beautiful furniture. If you'd just focus on it, you'd—"

"I'd what?" he spat out, causing Natalie to jump a bit. "Not be a drunk? Am I embarrassing you, dear daughter?"

Pausing a moment, Natalie knew tonight was not the night to talk sense into him. And she wasn't about to tell him that no one really knew she was his daughter, not with the different last name and the vague directions to where she lived.

She sighed. "I just thought you'd want to take pride in something, be able to show people you have more talents than just sports."

A grin crossed his face. "I know things didn't work out with your marriage, Natalie, but if you're going to say I need to get over being fired from the football team, you need to get over divorcing Craig after six months of marriage. Or your mama leaving the both of us to marry some rich investment banker. Or your grandmother leaving you on this earth to fend for yourself."

Heat rose to her face, and Natalie held back the tears. She fingered the small locket her grandmother had given her when she turned sixteen, something she'd worn every day since. Of all the accusations her father had flung her way, his last comment hurt the worst.

Grandma Tilly had been the one constant in Natalie's ever-changing world. And with the first anniversary of her death coming up in a matter of weeks, Natalie knew it was going to be tough, especially if her father continued to act so bitter and spiteful.

After her parent's divorce, Natalie and her mother had lived in Logan with Grandma Tilly in a beautiful home that had been built in the early 1900s. While her mom worked long hours, Grandma Tilly was always there to comfort and give sage wisdom.

Then, when Natalie's mother decided to marry Brent three years ago, it had been a major adjustment to the life of the three women, and it might have hurt even more had Grandma Tilly not been there to listen and comfort her. Even her broken marriage hadn't seemed as devastating with the words of the old woman.

What would Grandma Tilly say right now? Probably something about her thirty-year-old granddaughter needing to try her hand at dating once again. Natalie flicked away a tear before it had a chance to roll too far down and took a breath.

She would not cry in front of her father. Sure, they'd never had the best relationship, but she'd hoped to offer him some support when she moved back to Coldwater Creek. Dredging up her own past in the process was like a bucket of ice water dumped on her head. She gasped as if trying to pull in the air that wouldn't come.

"I moved back here to help you out and to get out of Cache Valley. We both have a past that would be easy to avoid, but every day is a lesson. I've moved on and am using my past mistakes to better myself. So don't go throwing everything in my face, or I'll do it to you!" She heard the finality in her voice and let her lips twitch up into a quick smile. Her grandmother would have cheered at that.

Her father's mouth hung open for several seconds before he closed it and nodded. "You're right. And I'm sorry. I haven't really told you how nice it's been to have someone else in this quiet house the past few months. And I'll not be saying anything more about what's done and over."

"Thank you." White flag raised, she'd have to find another way to get through to him about his own past and find out what really happened the night he got fired from the football team. But less drinking was certainly a start.

They sat that way for some time, and Natalie realized how much she'd missed the quiet of the small home in the mountains. She and her mother had lived just off Main Street from when she was eleven on, and the traffic always seemed to be there, no matter the time of day. With her mother moving to New York and her grandmother's passing, nothing had really kept her in Utah, and her father's health had been the perfect cover for the chance to mend herself in a new place with a clean slate.

The fact that she was several hours away from the man who betrayed her five years before was somewhat of a relief. Even after they'd gone their separate ways, it seemed that they always ended up in the same places, usually with his new wife on his arm. Just one more benefit to her sudden decision to settle down somewhere else.

As she thought about the things she was grateful for now that she was here, the handsome face from the hallway on Friday popped into her head. She had to be going crazy. She'd never obsessed over guys, and even with Craig, things were more businesslike than anything. There was some connection between her and the man in the hall, but she had no idea why.

Maybe it was the fact that he was forbidden fruit, now that she knew who he was. Easton McBride, painted as the evil villain in a story around the Hirsch home. But the kindness she'd seen in his eyes as he'd done all he could to help her start her car made her wonder if she'd really healed from all the scars of love and dating over the years.

"You haven't stored any newer batteries out in the garage, have you, Dad?" she asked, the memory of Easton bringing that to mind. Her dad had a mild hoarding problem when it came to scraps of wood and anything that had to do with an engine, and if she could save some money by getting one from there, she'd use it. At least until they got caught up on most of the past-due bills.

"I have a few I found at the junkyard a couple weeks back. What do you need it for?" Her dad stroked the thin beard that had grown back in the past few weeks. The staff in the emergency room had to shave it off in order to stitch a long gash back together from his chin to his cheekbone. It had been the first time she'd ever really seen her father without facial hair, and even with the thinner beard, he looked more like himself.

Natalie leaned her head back against the rocker. "My car wouldn't start after school on Friday. The guy who helped me jump it suggested I get a new battery, and I figured I'd ask before I go buy a new one."

"A guy, huh? Anyone I know?" Her father stood, a twinkle in his eye.

"Dad." She rolled her eyes, hoping to hide the panic and guilt she was feeling about her interaction with his enemy. "It was a quick encounter, and then I headed out to get home."

He waved her off. "I'll go test them and see which one will work best for you. I'd hate for you to spend money on something I've already got lying around."

Natalie smiled at his sudden enthusiasm. It had always been that way when she was younger, his interest in being able to use up every scrap possible. If only he could use that on a broader scale, like finances. But maybe that's why she was there, to make sure both of them survived through the new year.

CHAPTER 8

*I*t was just after lunch, and Easton was already exhausted from nearly a full day of work behind him. He'd been cleaning out pens and moving equipment for most of the morning, trying to get things all buttoned up for fall and the early winter that was supposed to set in within the next few weeks. They'd be moving cattle after the next game, and that took a lot of time away from the regular duties of the ranch. Anytime he could make things easier on his father, he did it.

Pulling up to the school in his old Ford pickup, he found a parking spot next to the line of reserved teacher spots. He slid the keys into his pocket as he got out and walked in the side door of Coldwater Creek High. A chill in the air caused him to shiver, and he was grateful for the warmth of the building as he stepped inside.

The halls were packed with students, all milling about for what must still be the lunch period. Easton pulled his phone from his pocket, checking the text Principal Jackson had sent earlier.

Reminder that the meeting for the Christmas Ball is in room

235 during 4th period. Please make sure you're there so you can help with any of the bigger items.

Easton was still unsure what exactly the man had meant by bigger items, but it was worth a bit of time to figure out what he needed to do. A small sacrifice of time to help out the Erickson family. He just hoped Johnny would be able to be at practice today.

The bell rang, bringing him back to the chaos as the noise from the students grew around him, their voices calling goodbyes as they walked down the halls. Taking the northeast staircase to the second floor, he read the classroom numbers as he went. He had to turn down one of the halls but finally found number 235 with no nameplate below it. He thought about going in but then decided against it, leaning against the wall across from the room. The lights were still off, and with the students waiting around it, the advisor probably wasn't back from lunch yet.

With his phone out, he scanned through various emails, seeing a few he still needed to respond to. Being one of the operators of a ranch was more time-consuming than most people thought, but in order to keep growing the opportunities for the ranch, he had to spend the time dealing with technology, especially since his father wanted nothing to do with anything online. So most of the billing, the emails, and inquiries all had to go through Easton when he could find the time. He might have to give up coaching football in the future or hire some kind of assistant if the ranch continued to increase.

The bell rang, and Easton tried to zone out the loud chatter moving past him as he plucked out an answer to one of the people from the cattle auction. By the time he pressed send, he looked up to see the door open and lights shining.

With the hallway mostly clear, Easton pushed off the wall and took the few steps to the door, peeking around the frame. When he saw the familiar woman from the parking lot on Friday, he paused, unsure of what to do. He'd thought about her off and on throughout the weekend, but he hadn't been able to find her in the crowd at the game. His ego had taken a hit, but was there ever really a possibility they could go well together?

"Coach, what are you doing here?" Talon asked, causing Easton to jump back a step.

"I, uh, well…" He cleared his throat and stepped through the doorway. His eyes glanced in the direction of Natalie, and she turned, her eyes going wide with surprise. "Principal Jackson said I was supposed to meet with you about the Christmas Ball? Am I in the right place?"

She blinked once or twice and nodded. "This is Student Council, and Principal Jackson made sure we were going to discuss the ball this afternoon. Please come in and join us, Mr. McBride."

"Easton, please. Mr. McBride is what everyone calls my father." He reached his hand forward, and her expression changed, making him glance down at his clothes to make sure nothing had been left on them from his work at the ranch earlier that day.

"The head football coach is gracing us with his presence to plan the ball? How did you get roped into this?" Natalie asked, her expression somber. The corners of her lips flickered a bit, and he wondered if that was supposed to be a jab or a flirtation. Just another reason he didn't understand women.

Easton shrugged, sliding into one of the desks next to Talon. He leaned over and whispered, "What are you doing in here?"

"I'm on the junior student council. I'm supposed to be here." Talon looked halfway between scared he was about to be punished and wondering what his coach was doing there.

"Let's get started, everyone." A girl with deep auburn hair stood from her desk and pulled a paper into her hands. "Okay, we'll have a recap of last Saturday's Harvest Dance for the first five minutes of this meeting and then move onto details for the ball."

Easton leaned back, already bored with the conversation. What was he even doing here? He glanced up and caught Natalie looking in his direction before she diverted it to look at the girl who was speaking. What was it about those eyes that intrigued him so much? It was like they had some hypnotizing power for him.

As the student recapping the previous dance wound down, ideas were thrown out about what the theme of the Christmas Ball should be. Easton chuckled at a few of them, earning himself a few unhealthy glares from Natalie.

"What if we do something like 'Deck the Halls' or something about mistletoe?" Talon offered.

Easton rolled his lips in to keep from bursting out laughing.

"Mistletoe could get a little dicey with parents, and we need to remember this is a fundraiser," Natalie said. "From what I've heard from our principal, we'll have more than just high school students and chaperones there, so you might not want to think about kissing your future dates at the dance." She smiled at the students, the action lighting up her entire face. Easton was impressed with how she let the students lead but offered her thoughts here and there.

"What about 'Winter Wonderland'?" the auburn-haired girl said. "I know it's probably common, but it would be easy and pretty to make everything white."

Several of the other students murmured agreements, and after a quick vote, they agreed on the theme.

"Are you sure you need me in here? We have to prepare

for our big rivals this week, and if you don't need me, I'll—" Easton said as he began to stand from his chair.

"Principal Jackson said we need your help with the venue, as well as several of the backdrops. Apparently, you have some experience with woodwork?" Natalie was looking down at some notes she'd made on a paper. When her light blue eyes looked up at him, he paused, unsure of what to do.

He shook his head and chuckled. "I helped put together some of the scenery for one of the plays a few years back. I'm not really the one with the skills, but one of my younger brothers is."

Easton's eyes were locked onto the teacher's, and he couldn't help but smile a bit as she didn't blink or look away.

After several charged seconds, she spoke. "However you get it done, that will work. Since you're so busy, we can discuss our designs and bring you some plans for them. Will that work?" She raised her eyebrows high.

Easton nodded, grateful he could escape. Their conversation was so stilted, different from the other day when he'd been working on her car.

When he'd just barely made it out the door, a hand grabbed his arm. He stopped and turned to find the attractive blonde woman standing before him.

"Look, I've never really had extra faculty support for a dance function, especially this early in the process. There are a lot of people who will be counting on this to be a grand event. I need to be able to trust that you'll do what you say you will." With her arms folded across her chest and her eyebrows raised, impatience glared in her eyes as she waited for his answer. Just like a typical high school teacher thinking they have all authority in all matters concerning the school.

A thread of irritation moved through Easton's upper body before he let it out in a long breath. He'd been the one to laugh at the students' suggestions, so he probably deserved her attitude. Trying to keep his voice even, he said, "I understand the importance of it, Ms. Lynch. We just met, and I seem to remember helping you out with your car. What would give you the idea that I don't keep my word?"

"Natalie."

Easton paused to make sure he'd heard what she'd just said before continuing his rant. "Two of the Ericksons are on my team, and I do all I can to protect those boys. If this is going to help them have the Christmas they deserve, I won't do anything to ruin it. Although, I'm unsure why you think I would do something like that."

Natalie's mouth moved, her lips opening and closing a few times like she was trying to form the words to speak. Finally, she said, "I appreciate that. I'll make sure Talon brings you any information once we've made some decisions." With that, she turned on her heel and stalked back into the classroom.

That hadn't gone remotely close to how he'd planned it. But at least he could go over a few minutes of film before practice started.

Walking past the large open window looking out to the east part of the parking lot, Easton saw several dark clouds rolling in. It was going to be another wet day of practice.

As he jogged down the stairs, Principal Jackson was turning onto the landing. "Easton, I thought you'd be helping plan the ball." His tone was casual, but the narrowed eyes signaled otherwise.

"I was just there, sir. They've decided on a theme and will contact me when they need more help. Did you tell them I do woodworking?" Easton asked, one foot on a stair lower than the other as he waited for the man's response.

The principal's face softened a bit, and he nodded. "I remember you doing a great job for that one musical a few years ago. I can't recall the name of it at the moment, but I think you'd be able to handle cutting a few pieces of plywood, right?"

"My brother Hunter is the master of woodworking. Me, not so much. But I'll see if he has time to help me with it."

"Good to hear. Make sure you spend time on this, especially once the season is over. I know you're already stretched, but getting the lodge to the point where it can be used for this function will help out the school."

Easton nodded. The lodge. Something he had no control over and wasn't the owner of. "I'll stop by and see my brother tonight."

The man grinned and disappeared up the stairs. Why did accepting an assignment like this have to become so time-consuming? With the playoffs just a few weeks away and getting things ready with the animals and ranch for winter, he realized this was going to be a bigger job than he'd originally thought, especially if people kept breathing down his neck.

Easton would make it work. He had to, or else his mother would scold him for accepting something and then not following through. And leaving a family without much to celebrate on their Christmas.

Feeling the exhaustion pile onto his shoulders, he breathed out and walked into the guys' locker room. He'd have to be more careful about accepting any assignment not clearly laid out for him in the future.

CHAPTER 9

Of all the people the principal would assign to help out, it had to be Easton McBride. Natalie groaned as she tried to focus on the essay in front of her the following afternoon. It was Talon's, and he'd miraculously gotten it to her by the end of the day last week like he'd promised. Maybe all athletes weren't so bad, but she still had to be careful to not give in too much.

It was probably the fact that Talon was a football player that made her keep thinking of Easton's handsome face, the chocolate-brown irises that could probably see right through her to her soul.

Why was she obsessing over him already? He was off-limits. He'd gotten her father fired. She couldn't be thinking there was any chance at a future between the two of them. And he was probably just like her ex, which was something she didn't need to relive. She would put her head down and focus on upping the percentage of the kids passing the AP test this year. That would keep her busy enough to not worry about the head football coach. At least, she hoped it would.

Her phone rang, pulling her out of the round of thoughts

that seemed to never diverge from the man's gorgeous dimple. Even when he wasn't smiling, there was a hint of it there, and Natalie had learned long ago that a dimple was one of her weaknesses when it came to men.

"Hello?" she answered, without looking at the screen first.

"Natalie, are you on your way home yet?" her father's rusty voice managed. He'd been coming down with a cold the night before, and now he could barely speak.

She glanced up at the clock, seeing it was almost five. "I'm just packing up to leave. What do you need, Dad?"

"I just realized I'm out of my blood pressure medicine. Can you swing by the pharmacy and pick it up?"

"Sure. I'll head out before they close." She said goodbye and hung up before quickly dialing the number for the pharmacy. They closed earlier than she was used to in Utah, and she needed to get the medicine processing so she wouldn't have to wait longer there than necessary.

Grabbing her coat and her purse, she walked out into the hall with long strides as she gave all the information to the pharmacy tech. Going over her evening, she tried to think of what they would have for dinner. She'd forgotten to get out some of the meat in the freezer that morning while rushing to make it to school on time after getting all the animals fed on the small piece of land they owned.

While she was at the store, she might as well pick up a few of the other groceries as well. She missed the order-online option of the bigger city, as she'd been able to save a lot of time that way, but this small town didn't look to be getting that program anytime soon. Many of the townsfolk enjoyed bumping into one another at the grocery store and chatting the day away. But since Natalie didn't know many people here, she didn't have to worry about that so much.

Driving her compact car down the highway, she turned on some of her favorite songs from a decade ago. She pulled out the pencil she'd used to pull her hair up and rolled the window down, taking a deep breath of the fall breeze. The colors had already changed some time ago, but there were those leaves still hanging on to the trees that made it all beautiful, despite the large bald patches.

She parked at the grocery store and ran in, her small heels clacking against the ground with each step. Seeing the pickup line, she stood in line behind the fifth customer, breathing a sigh of relief that she'd made it there before things closed up. They couldn't turn her away now, right?

"Natalie, it's good to see you again." That deep voice caused her head to snap up, staring into the face of the man she'd been daydreaming of for the past hour. She hadn't noticed it was him in front of her.

Her cheeks heated, and she looked back down, trying to pretend she was digging for something in her purse. Not wanting to be rude, she said, "Easton. Not out practicing to beat your rivals?" The fact that she'd just used his words against him made her smile, curious as to his answer.

"My mother asked me to get her prescriptions. What about you?" Easton stood with his eyes locked onto her face, his hands stuffed into his pockets.

Natalie looked away as soon as she saw that it accentuated the look of his biceps under his plaid short-sleeved shirt. What was a guy doing wearing something like that when it felt like ten degrees outside?

"Hmm…oh, I just had to pick up something for my, uh, neighbor." She couldn't outright tell him she was the daughter of the guy he'd helped get fired. The lie sounded lame to her ears, but Easton nodded and smiled at her.

"Sounds like you're adapting to Coldwater Creek well. Helping out neighbors should be the town theme."

"He has a hard time getting into town, so I help out when I can. Are you going to be ready for your game this week?"

she asked, hoping to change the subject as quickly as possible. Why she went with the sport she now loathed, she wasn't sure.

Easton nodded, glancing back at the line and taking a step forward. "Yeah, we ran a bunch of the new plays, and I let the kids out early. They've been working hard, and I don't want them to get behind on their schoolwork."

A football coach who cared about an athlete's grades? That was a new one. "How long have you been coaching for Coldwater Creek, Easton?" Natalie folded her arms across her chest, trying not to smile at how this sounded more like an interrogation than a casual conversation.

"Five years. I played under Coach Calhoun, and when he got sick, they asked me to take over. I've loved every minute of it, even though it's tough juggling work and coaching most of the time."

"What is it you do for work?" She knew little more than what she'd learned about the family when she was growing up, that they owned a ranch. But past that, she didn't know a whole lot about each of the McBride individuals. Other than her father's opinions of them had tainted her own.

Easton shrugged and took another step forward. Only three more people to go. "I'm in training to take over the ranch from my father."

Natalie smiled as she said, "Just in training, huh?" Was she suddenly flirting? She shook her head slightly, hoping to get all the right brain cells back where they should be.

"Well, my dad is slowing down, but it's difficult to get him to be done completely. I've been ranching since I was little, so I know most of the ins and outs, but I have to say that doing marketing and all the office work eats up a lot of my time."

"Ah, the son of a rancher who has to take over all the technology-related stuff. I can sympathize with that." There were days when she wanted to throw her phone across the room after checking their social media, wondering if things would ever improve. At least they were getting more calls and inquiries about the horse-training program, but no actual contracts yet.

"Really? I guess I pictured that a gal from Utah would have parents in some kind of corporate world."

Natalie laughed a bit. "My mom is, kind of. She was a paralegal for a big law firm down there. She married a guy, and they moved east. From what I hear, she doesn't really have to work anymore."

"And what about your dad?" His eyes were so earnest, so sincere, and Natalie had a hard time looking away.

"My dad has other pursuits, but sometimes it's keeping him focused that's the biggest problem." She closed her mouth, surprised she'd said anything at all. Easton was so easy to talk to, which made the version her father had told her seem like a completely different person. And she wasn't usually this open with close friends, let alone strangers.

Easton moved forward once again, only one person at the window before him. "Would you be interested in having dinner with me sometime? Maybe tomorrow night? I'll be done with practice and can pick you up around six thirty." He gave her a half-grin, popping the dimple. How could she say no to that?

"Um, let's see. Tomorrow is Wednesday." She paused, trying to think of a reason to not go out with the guy who was starting to crumble all the opinions she'd had of him prior. "I should be okay with that. But tell me the place, and I'll meet you there."

"Are you sure? It's no trouble to pick you up."

As much as she wanted to give in, everyone in town knew where her father lived, and she couldn't risk a fight breaking out between the two of them. She'd have to find a way to tell

Easton who her father was. Maybe then he'd tell her his side of the story. After all they'd talked about over the past little while, she'd be interested in hearing what he thought of the whole thing. Then maybe she'd feel less guilty about being attracted to him behind her father's back.

"I have to run a few errands after school, so it will be easier to just meet you when I'm done."

They traded phone numbers, and he said with a smile, "I'll text you the place." He then turned and moved up to the counter of the pharmacy.

Natalie shouldn't have felt so excited about a date with Easton McBride, but there was something about him that made her want to get to know him better. He seemed different than most of the athletes and football players she'd known growing up, even different than Craig, the football player she'd actually married for half a year. Maybe it was possible to love that sport again, just as she had so many years before when she'd been to every football game, watching her father do what he loved before her parents' divorce.

As Easton waved goodbye and left the store, her thoughts swirled around everything that had transpired that day, the conversation they'd had in line and the excitement of the next day. She couldn't get her hopes up. He was just being nice and inviting the new girl out to dinner, right?

CHAPTER 10

*E*aston had a big smile on his face the whole ride home to the ranch. It had been an interesting day, but the highlight had been getting the frosty layer to melt from Natalie's personality. The idea to ask her on a date surprised even him, as it had been a while since he'd dated anyone. But she'd said yes, at least to meeting him wherever he decided.

He hadn't questioned before where she lived, nor had any of the gossips divulged that information. In a small town like this, there weren't many places to live without the rest of the world knowing it. Maybe she lived up in one of the rental cabins in the mountains. She seemed like the reserved type at first but now he was just excited to get to know her better.

He tried to think of different places he could take her, maybe on a picnic somewhere. He shook his head at that one. The late-October chill was already setting in, and they'd freeze if they sat outside to eat. There were a lot of local restaurants they could enjoy, but for some reason, he wanted to keep the dinner more intimate, hoping to learn all he could about her without being interrupted by the townsfolk.

An idea popped into his head, and he grinned from ear to ear. He turned off the highway just after the bend and pulled down the driveway of Silver Brook Lodge. Shifting into park, he turned off his truck and made his way over to the main building. Opening the back door, he called out, "Walk? Walker? Are you home?"

"In here," came a voice from what sounded like the kitchen.

Easton took several steps down the hall and turned the corner, having visited this place several times while it was under construction. He found his brother sitting behind the counter with a plate of meat and potatoes in front of him.

"That looks good enough to eat," Easton said, sitting down next to him.

"I am definitely enjoying it. What brings you here?" Walker cut a piece of meat and stuffed it into his mouth before looking back up at Easton.

"Do you think I could have dinner with someone here tomorrow night?" Easton felt a part of his chest constrict, like this was his last chance of having a great first date with Natalie Lynch.

Walker's eyebrows rose higher than Easton had ever seen, and his mouth opened and shut as if he couldn't form the words to respond.

"We'd just use the kitchen, and I'd make sure everything is cleaned up."

"Meaning you'll have Mom make the food and just bring it here." He sat back in his chair, his hands folded behind his head as he took in a deep breath. "Yeah, I guess you can. What time? I've got the guys coming to finish some of the wiring upstairs tomorrow."

"About six thirty."

Walker nodded. "That should work. So, who is this girl? I know it's been a while, but weren't you just saying the other day that to get you to date again would be quite a feat?" He smiled, the look taunting Easton.

"There's something about her that just makes me want to get to know her more. She's the new English teacher at the school. I have to help her and the committee with the Christmas Ball."

"Ah, wooing the new English teacher. This should be interesting."

Easton punched his brother in the shoulder, sick of the teasing already. Sure, Easton's dating life was far from perfect, and he hadn't been on a date in a few years, but he had to start somewhere. It wasn't like Walker's love life was all that exciting either. He'd been single since his ex-fiancée had run off with another bull rider, causing Walker to be less enthusiastic about the opposite sex.

"It's one date. Just give a guy a break every once in a while, will you?"

Raising his hands in surrender, Walker said, "Sorry, I have to get a few jabs in here and there. You've been single a lot longer than I have, so I just wanted to make sure you were up for a first date."

"We'll see how it goes. If she has a sister, I'll work to set you up."

"I'm good. My relationship is with this lodge right now. Just trying to get everything in line for the opening in December is keeping me on my toes. I won't have time for a girl until a couple of years from now."

Easton stood, his stomach rumbling a bit. "Well, let me know how I can help you out with it. Principal Jackson is all over me to make sure things go well for the ball."

Walker chuckled. "I knew he'd be worried about it. I've already got guests signed up to stay here a week before the dance, so I should be done in time for the ball."

"That's what I like to hear," Easton said, slapping his

brother on the shoulder. "I better head back. I'm sure Dad will be antsy about the night chores, and I still haven't eaten."

"I'd offer you some food, but this is all I cooked. Besides, Mom will have made real mashed potatoes instead of the instant kind."

Turning his nose up at that, Easton nodded. "I'll see you tomorrow, brother. Let me know how I can return the favor."

He left the house before Walker could respond and jumped into his truck. He'd have to delicately talk to his mother about what to make for dinner the next day. As nice as it sounded to have her make it and then him just take it to the lodge, he wanted to impress Natalie a bit, hoping to move through the outer wall she seemed to have put up, especially when he'd said he'd pick her up.

He just hoped he could keep the secret of his date from his younger sisters. Molly, his youngest sibling, was a senior at Coldwater Creek, and she probably had Natalie as her English teacher. Letting her know about the one date would be like telling the high school gossip queen to spread the news like wildfire, which would only alert the adult gossips.

Best to keep this all to himself and see where things went after their date.

CHAPTER 11

*N*atalie had been somewhat nervous all through school, forgetting her train of thought often while teaching. By the time the final bell rang, she breathed a sigh of relief. She hadn't been on a kind-of-date in years, and that last one had been a complete disaster, mostly on her part.

She made it out to her car several minutes later, the line to exit the parking lot shorter than she'd expected. Glancing out to the football field before she got into her car, her heart rate sped up, thinking of Easton standing out there and waiting for his players to arrive for practice.

Her hands fidgeted with the radio as she moved down the highway. She still hadn't received a text from him, and she hoped he wasn't canceling now.

What was she thinking? Just because the guy was very attractive and kind didn't mean things would work out. As much as she'd always secretly wanted her own happily ever after, it had seemed like luck wasn't on her side ever since her divorce from Craig.

Shaking off the fear that Easton would stand her up, she just had to get ready and see what happened.

She was nearly home when her phone pinged, and she punched the accelerator, curious as to who would have texted her. Sometimes she wondered why she even carried a phone because the only person who seemed to contact her anymore was her father. Her mother had called once before school started, but life had changed in a whirlwind, and she didn't have the time for Natalie like she used to. The call she missed most was from Grandma Tilly, reassuring her she could handle anything life threw her way.

She'd barely put the car in park before she reached over and grabbed her phone. Her home screen lit up with a message, Easton's name at the top of it.

Sorry, I was planning things last night and then got busy this morning. Meet me at the Silver Brook Lodge. Come hungry

Natalie read the message a couple more times, a hesitant smile showing some of the excitement she felt. She really needed to resist the urge to overanalyze, but those instincts seemed to uncover themselves from their long slumber.

She got out of the car, wondering who was rebuilding the old lodge that had burned down when she was a small child and why they were meeting there. She hadn't been to that end of the Coldwater Creek Valley since she moved back.

After a quick shower and doing her hair, she worked on her makeup, trying to make it subtle but enough to accentuate her features. She picked out a white glittery blouse and a pair of dark jeans, pairing them with her knee-high brown boots. After a little bit of lip gloss, she was ready to go, and from the look at her watch, she knew she needed to head out now.

When she walked into the front room, her father looked up at her, staring. "Where are you going all dressed up?"

She hadn't taken the chance to come up with a story, but

she did what she could to think fast. "Um, one of the teachers at school is having a small get-together. I should be back around eight thirty or nine."

Her father looked at her a few seconds longer and then nodded. "Have a good time, honey."

"No alcohol, Dad. You still need to feed the animals tonight."

Anger passed across his face in a wave, then he nodded again with a somber look. "I'll make sure they're fed."

She leaned down and kissed his cheek, waving goodbye before she headed out the door and back into her car. Taking slow breaths, she drove down the winding road that led back into town.

As she got closer and closer to their meeting place, Natalie's hands began to sweat, and her stomach clenched. Would she be able to make it through a dinner with someone she barely knew? She just hoped she wouldn't make a complete fool out of herself in the process.

But she also couldn't get attached to this guy. She'd use this date as a practice, some kind of warm-up to getting herself back in the dating game. There probably weren't too many men her age in Coldwater Creek, so her pickings would be slim, but dating Easton was not an option, at least not more than tonight.

But she could find a way to be friends with him, right? She'd been friends with plenty of guys in college, until Craig had driven them all away, claiming he wanted all her attention to himself.

As soon as she turned into the driveway of where the map on her phone had directed her, she was surprised by the beauty of the massive log cabin. She recognized the small cabins lined up behind the lodge, but they'd been spruced up with some stain and new chinking between the logs.

She parked next to Easton's truck and slipped out, noticing the lack of other cars in the parking lot. Staring at the ground for a few seconds, she was grateful she'd chosen wedges instead of heels now that she saw all the gravel between her and the front door. Natalie had never been the most graceful person, and while she was confident in heels for the most part, she knew her own limits—and gravel was one of them.

Approaching the front door, she admired the light shining through the windows. The sun had almost set, and the last few rays of gold tinged the darkening sky, causing the warmth of the lights to draw her in.

She knocked on the door, anxious nerves sifting through her. What was she doing? She was so far out of practice when it came to a dinner date. How would she survive without acting like an idiot? She could give the cold shoulder, pretend like she didn't really care about any of this. But that would be more suited for a restaurant where other people would be, not when he'd set up something as intimate as this.

Just as she was ready to turn and bolt back to the car, the door opened, and Easton grinned at her, throwing a towel over his shoulder. He wore a light-blue button-up shirt with the sleeves rolled up to his elbows, and against his olive skin, it had her insides flipping. Why did the man have to look so good?

"I'm so glad you made it. Come in and warm up." He opened the door for her, allowing her to walk past him. He smelled like a mixture of fall and pasta, both of which made her knees go a little weak.

Focusing on each step, she still stumbled as his hand rested on her lower back, gently guiding her. He caught her from falling to the ground, but their faces were only inches apart, causing her mind to spin. The smile on his face was small, but his eyes searched hers as if looking for the answer to some unspoken question.

After several seconds, he lifted her to a standing position, for which she was grateful since every part of her body had frozen at his touch.

"Are you okay? I hope I didn't scare you." His face showed his worry, and Natalie had to take several calming breaths.

Waving it off, she said, "I'm fine. I just have trouble walking normally sometimes." She paused and made a point to sniff the air, hoping it would distract from the awkwardness she felt. "It smells delicious. What did you make?"

He smiled. "It's a surprise."

His hand slid back to the small of her back, and this time she focused on moving forward, conscious of the electricity pulsing from his warm hand. She'd never felt like this with Craig, but then again, he'd never done much to help guide her anywhere. She liked the safety she felt from it and was a little disappointed when they arrived in the kitchen and he moved to the stove to stir something in a pot.

"Go ahead and have a seat on one of the barstools. I'm sorry it's not a regular table. My brother Walker has been working to rebuild this place since he quit bull riding, and while it's getting there, there are still a lot of things that need to be finished."

Looking around, Natalie noticed the detail of the trim and all the touches just in the kitchen. "This place is amazing. What was here before?" She tried to act innocent, like she really was some girl who'd never lived in Coldwater Creek, curious as to Easton's answer.

"There used to be a lodge here with a big steakhouse. But it burned down about twenty years ago, and the owner never had the money to rebuild. He rented out the little cabins in the back for quite a while, but things just kept going downhill. Walker was trying to decide what to do after the rodeo and made an offer on the place. He's spent the past ten months trying to get it all fixed up and ready for business." Easton turned to the sauce and stirred a minute before looking back at Natalie. "I think this town is more excited than he is to have another restaurant."

"That is one thing I do miss from Utah. So many places to eat out, I never felt any pressure to cook if I didn't want to. Totally different story here."

A timer dinged on the stove, and Easton moved to turn it off. He slipped on an oven mitt and pulled a glass baking dish out of the oven. "I hope you like pasta, because I made chicken parmesan."

Natalie blinked a few times. Wow, he was really going over the top with this. She'd suspected pasta, but the fact that it wasn't just a jar of spaghetti sauce dumped over some noodles was causing her attraction to him to go from wow to who was this guy? Rancher, football coach, and has the ability to cook something that doesn't need direct instructions on the box?

"I'm a fan of food, especially the kind I don't have to cook." She grinned at him, and he winked at her, causing that adorable dimple to sink in. She was flirting, and she needed to cool it down. She could be good friends with him, right? There wasn't a law against that, even in her father's household. But she knew that after tonight, she was going to have to work to keep her emotions tucked deep down so even she wouldn't notice them.

He plated the chicken and noodles, adding a large scoop of pasta sauce on top. He slid it over to her and retrieved two smaller plates from a large cabinet next to the hood of the stove. "Here is a plate for your salad, and here are the dressings I have." He pulled out Italian and ranch from the fridge, sliding them over on the counter. He also grabbed the green parmesan bottle and walked around her to sit on the barstool next to her.

"Wow, you've gone all out for this. Thank you." Natalie smiled at him, pulling the salad bowl closer to her. She grabbed the tongs and dished up some of the colorful salad and then opened the bottle of ranch, allowing herself a generous helping.

Easton reached over and grabbed a loaf of French bread she hadn't seen on the other side of the large counter, setting the cutting board with the pieces and a small container of butter in between them.

"Can't forget the bread with the pasta." He grinned at her, taking the bowl of salad and dishing out his own.

After a blessing on the food, Natalie took several bites of the salad and then the chicken. "There's no way you made this all yourself." She waved her fork over the entire meal and looked at him, hoping her expression was challenging enough against the draw of those brown eyes.

"I had a few pointers, but yes, I made it myself. Walker had to run into town to get some supplies for his electricians, so I've just been here for the last hour, getting things ready."

She shook her head. "Well, this is all incredible. I'm going to need your recipe."

He bit his lip, looking a bit sheepish. "I'll take a picture of it. My mom wrote down all the ingredients and steps."

A pang of jealousy whipped across her chest, and she did her best to give him a bright smile. Her mother had done a lot of that for her growing up, giving her tips, helping her work through problems. And she had more recipes in her grandmother's handwriting than fit into her small ring binder. But she hadn't dug it out of one of the boxes she'd brought with her when she moved. She made a mental note to do just that so they could have a little more variety than taco soup and boxed dinners.

"She sounds like a great mother, then."

They both ate in silence for a time before Easton's questions began.

"What brought you to Coldwater Creek? I can imagine we aren't as lively here as the city or suburbs." His gaze was so focused that Natalie looked down, subconsciously wiping her face with her napkin.

"A lot happened to me in the last year, and as much as I tried to get through it, the past just seemed to keep showing up everywhere I went. So when I saw an opening here, I applied, hoping it would be the chance for me to get a fresh start."

"Was there more than just your mother getting married?" Easton asked, taking a bite of chicken from his fork.

Blowing out a breath, Natalie debated for several seconds whether she should share everything with this near perfect stranger. But maybe her past would be a repellent on his part.

"I was married for a little bit several years ago. But he cheated on me, and we got divorced." She said the words slowly, watching his face for a reaction. His eyebrows rose, but that was the extent to his surprise. "He wasn't the guy I'd dated for so long, and he started telling me things that no new bride should ever have to hear." Her mind switched gears, pulling on every heartstring she had.

"My grandmother died last December, and she was pretty close to the best friend I've ever had." She moved her hand up and rubbed the locket around her neck, staring straight ahead as she tried to calm the tidal wave of emotions slamming into her chest.

Using her napkin to wipe at the corner of her eyes, she was surprised when his arm wrapped around the back of her, pulling her into him a little bit. He didn't say anything, just held her as the tears slipped out silently.

After a minute or two, she got control of her emotions and sat back up, trying to smile at him. "Thank you. I'm sorry to be such a downer, especially after all the work you put into this."

"Natalie," he said, his voice soft and tender. "We all have a past that isn't the best. Don't worry about it. I'm just glad you felt comfortable enough to share that with me."

His words called to her curiosity, and she asked, "What about your past relationships?"

He closed his eyes, and the side of his mouth ticked up. "I walked right into that one, didn't I?" The two of them chuckled a bit before his face sobered. "I haven't had a serious girlfriend since college. With football and then coming back here to the ranch, there always seemed to be more important things than a relationship for me. My schedule gets pretty crazy, especially at certain times of the year, and I feel like I wouldn't be able to give it my all, you know?"

"I can understand that. What made you decide to ask me out tonight, then?" The words were out before Natalie could stop them, and she focused on buttering her bread.

Without missing a beat, he said, "I thought it would be fun getting to know you better."

For a few seconds, silence settled over them as Natalie waited for him to say more. Then, with a wry smile, she said, "Or I'm just the new meat in this small town?"

Easton frowned and shook his head. "No, there is a certain mystery to you, and I'll admit I'm a bit curious."

The rest of the dinner melted into lighter topics, more of the typical "getting to know you" questions, but Natalie was still surprised that he'd shared so much about his life with her and vice versa. Easton was so easy to talk to, and she could see that even though it had been several years since his career ended, there were still some regrets there.

Once the dinner was finished and they'd cleaned up the dishes, Easton asked, "Would you like to watch a movie?"

Glancing into the cozy great room of the lodge, Natalie was being pulled in two directions with her emotions. She finally shook her head.

"Maybe another time. I have to work tomorrow, and with all the chores in the morning, I've been cutting it too close to the final bell."

Easton laughed. "I can understand that one. Do you live on a ranch or farm?"

Her mind scrambled, trying to find some excuse or plausible explanation. "Um, well, my landlord has a bunch of horses. I get a discount on my rent if I feed and take care of them."

He looked curious, like he was going to prod for more information, but Natalie pulled her jacket from the rack by the door and turned the knob, making a quick exit.

Easton walked her to her car, and Natalie half hoped, half dreaded the idea of him kissing her there under the bright moonlit sky. He opened her door, and before he could do anything, she leaned in and gave him a hug, breathing in that same smell of the outdoors.

"Thank you for everything tonight," she said, pulling away and sliding into her car. She didn't dare look up at him until he'd shut the door, and she waved as she pulled out of the drive, her heart acting like a runaway horse.

Shaking her head, she said, "Natalie, girl, we've got to chill out. Remember, that was just a practice run." But even telling herself that did little good. An image of him holding her as they swayed along a dance floor popped into her mind.

A practice date that was going to be hard to top for any other guy she dated in the future. Her heart was starting to tell her she wanted it to be Easton. She was in trouble.

CHAPTER 12

As if he'd been lying in wait until Natalie left, Walker pulled into the driveway just as she pulled out of it. Easton had hoped to get away without a bunch of questions. He already knew his mother would be full of them once he arrived home, but talking about a date with his brother right now felt like the most awkward thing that could happen that evening.

"How did it go?" Walker asked, stepping out of his even more beat-up pickup. Easton knew how frugal his brother was and that buying the land and restoring the lodge didn't affect what he'd worked hard to earn while part of the rodeo circuit.

"It went well. Thanks for letting me use your place. It's pretty amazing here. You've done a great job, Walk."

"Don't try to change the subject. Did you have a good time? Will there be another date?"

Easton chewed on the side of his cheek, reflecting on the events of the evening. "I hope so. We just seemed to click about a lot of things. She's been married before, which was somewhat of a shock at first. But it only lasted a few months, so I guess that isn't anything to fuss over."

"That's a new one. Are you okay with that?"

"I thought it would be weird, but I just kind of listened to her. Sounds like he was verbally abusive or something, and he cheated on her. Her mom got remarried, and her grandmother died this past December, so it sounds like she's been through a lot in the past few years. But it was a first date. Don't go trying to plan my bachelor party." He grinned at Walker and slugged him in the arm.

"Sounds good. I hope it works out for you, man." Walker reached into his truck and pulled out a couple of bags that looked to be full of electrical supplies and outlets. "I ran into Old Man Hirsch at the store. He gave me the eye as I walked by and then said something under his breath I couldn't quite catch, but I heard your name. Sounds like you're still on his hit list."

Easton rolled his eyes. "I've done everything I can to talk to him, but he just accuses me of being the one to get him fired from coaching. I still don't think he can remember much of that night, and it's gotten to the point that I'm like, 'Whatever.' As long as I stay away from him, we'll both be happy, right?"

"You're taking it really well. I thought you hated the man."

"Dislike strongly," Easton corrected. "He was always bugged that I got the head coaching position over him, especially after being one of the coaches when I was in high school. But because I had him escorted out of the game for being drunk, it made him hate me even more. Oh well, though. At least I haven't run into him for a while, though the gossips still tell me when he's been spreading rumors around town about me. Does he still live up the canyon?"

"As far as I know. He's got a few more horses now, from

what I've heard around town. Maybe he'll go back to what he's great at and forget everything that happened."

"Fat chance of that." Easton smirked. "I better get home. I've got to get up early tomorrow again. We have to drive up to northern Wyoming to play on Friday, and I'm hoping to get a practice in on our field before we head out on the bus."

Walker held his hand up for a high five. "Good luck, Coach. Go beat them Aztecs!"

Walking around to his truck, Easton slid inside and turned the ignition. He rolled down his window and said, "If you need help around the lodge on Saturday, I should be home around noon and can help you then."

"I'll plan on you. I need all the help I can get to have this place ready for reservations come December."

"Especially the school Christmas Ball. I'm supposed to keep on top of you, thanks to Principal Jackson." He grinned mischievously and pointed at Walker. "He's worried it won't be done."

Walker groaned. "Yeah, him and most of the town. Go dream of your teacher and let me worry about the lodge."

Easton took off with a laugh, his mind moving back to the conversation of the evening. Every time he'd touched Natalie, he'd felt sparks fly through his fingertips and up to his chest. As much as he tried to brush it off as a result of a first date after over ten years of singleness, something about her kept pulling his thoughts.

Especially to the moment when she'd stumbled and he'd caught her in his arms. He'd been tempted to kiss her but was afraid that if he did, she'd just turn and walk right back out of the lodge. To be honest, he was still surprised she'd even shown up after the cold shoulder he'd felt a few times after she'd found out his name.

He made a mental note to ask her about that the next time he saw her. There was so much about Natalie Lynch he didn't know, but the urge to get to know her grew stronger with each thought of her. She seemed like a good woman, someone to stick by his side and work through a lot of things with. But then again, her marriage hadn't lasted. What had triggered the change? Was she just telling him what he wanted to hear?

Pushing that all aside, he focused on the barrage of questions he was about to get from his mother. He just hoped she didn't mention anything about being on her way to finally getting grandkids. That was his limit.

CHAPTER 13

When Natalie pulled up to her house, the sky was a dark navy blue and a few lights shone from the house. For some reason, they weren't as inviting as the ones from the lodge had been. She just hoped her father was in a decent mood. She didn't have the strength to deal with any messes or arguments.

She found him sitting in the recliner he usually occupied, watching a playoff baseball game.

"How was your night, Dad?" she asked, sitting on the love seat next to him.

He looked over at her with hooded eyes, and Natalie discreetly tried to see if they were bloodshot.

"It was good, my girl. I just went down to the hardware store. We were all out of light bulbs, and I needed to get out for a minute." He paused a moment and focused on the TV as if the conversation was over. And then he spoke again, saying, "I saw that McBride boy there, the second oldest one."

Natalie couldn't breathe, knowing that when her father saw any of the McBrides, things tended to go bad. "Please tell me you just moved to another part of the store."

"I didn't do anything to him, just said his brother is a filthy liar who doesn't deserve to be the head football coach." Her father spat out the last few words, causing Natalie to jump back a bit in surprise.

Groaning, she stood up, the anger and frustration welling up in her. "Dad, this is high school football we're talking about. You make thousands on training horses in just a few months. You'd have to work for thirty years to make that kind of money being the football coach. Can't you just leave it alone? Move on with your life?"

Fire ignited in her father's eyes. "Have you switched sides? Because you should know by now that blood is thicker than water."

"I'm still on your side, Dad. But I want you to move on, get a new life goal. You've always wanted to train a horse good enough for the Kentucky Derby. Why can't we focus on that instead of what happened a few years ago?" She puckered her lips, hoping that she hadn't given away the fact that she'd been with Easton that evening or of her growing feelings for him.

If there was a way to find out what had really happened the night her father was arrested, the easier it would be to get this all resolved.

"I'd like to get to that point. But I can't go into town now without everyone looking at me like I'm some kind of enemy. I didn't do anything wrong." Her dad ground his back teeth together.

"Do you remember that night, Dad? What happened?" He was already agitated enough that she shouldn't be trying to press the issue, but she was sick of the tiptoeing around certain subjects.

His face turned to hers, his eyes like stone as he saw her but also saw past her. "It was the anniversary of you and your mama leaving me. I thought I'd treat myself to a few drinks down at the bar, hoping to get rid of some of the pain. When I woke up after a couple hours, I was in the town jail. The next thing I knew, I was being relieved of my coaching duties at the request of Easton McBride. One of the cops told me he was the one who called it in."

Natalie knew how belligerent her father could get, so maybe Easton had done it as a way to keep everyone safe. Or maybe it was a way to get him off the coaching staff. Either way, she needed to stay as neutral as possible about it all without her father catching on. She wanted to help the situation, but having her father distrust her wasn't going to help.

She'd gotten her father's side of things, but how was she going to get Easton's side without him knowing who she was related to? That was the convenience of still carrying her ex's last name. Most of the town still didn't know she was a Hirsch.

"I'll let you rest, Dad. I've got to get to bed so I can get up at a normal hour tomorrow." She kissed him on the cheek and moved down the hall into her bedroom. She thought about her evening with Easton. Things felt so easy and free, nothing like she'd ever had at the start of a relationship before. Could it really be that easy?

Lying in her bed, she stared up at the ceiling, which still held the glow-in-the-dark stars from when she was a kid. If only she could get a direct sign about what she should do, that would make her life easier. But then again, that was part of the journey of life.

She'd had a great time with Easton, but that was all it could be, at least until she knew the truth. She was surprised at how much she wanted to know it now, just so she might spend more time with the handsome football coach.

CHAPTER 14

Natalie had slept well on Friday night, going to bed soon after receiving the last text from Easton. They'd won their game in a nail-biter ending, going into overtime and winning on a field goal. Then he'd asked her to go to the Halloween carnival in the town square the next evening. She'd debated saying yes because most of the town attended the festivities from what she could remember and she was still apprehensive for word to get back to her father.

I'll go with you. I just need to make sure I get all my papers graded before then.

Is there anything I can do to help with that?

His quip made her laugh out loud, and since she'd been eating breakfast next to her dad when she reread it Saturday morning, he'd given her a strange look.

No, I'll just meet you around town when I'm done.

She was falling for this guy, and the thought of her father finding out gnawed at her conscience. But what filled her with guilt was the fact that he still didn't know she was the daughter of Darryl Hirsch. She had to tell him, but would that end her chances of hanging out with him more? It was a selfish thought, but she didn't want this to end, not yet anyway.

After a morning spent pulling weeds in the garden and brushing many of the horses, she moved back inside to grade papers. But she'd forgotten to bring them home, meaning she had to run to the school.

She was on her way out of the building when she spotted the school buses that had transported the football players home. As she was about to turn a corner, she heard a familiar deep voice, causing her to pause. She peeked around it, seeing Easton talking to one of his players. The young man looked familiar, but Natalie was still trying to remember names in her own classes, let alone all the rest of the school.

"Do you need a ride home?" Easton asked.

"Probably. I'm not sure whose house I'm supposed to be at this weekend, and if I call either one of my parents, they'll blame the other."

"Go get in my truck. I'll make sure everyone else has a way home, and then we'll figure out where you need to be. Has the divorce been finalized yet?"

From Natalie's angle, all she could see was the sadness and disappointment on the kid's face.

He shook his head. "No, they can't agree on much, so my sister and I just get shuffled from one house to the other until they can decide."

Easton placed a hand on the player's shoulder. "If you ever need anything, you have my number, right?"

"Yes, sir."

"Make sure to use it. I can imagine how rough it would be to be stuck in the middle. You will be able to do great things, Sam. You just have to believe that." Easton pulled him in for a backslapping hug and then sent him off to the truck.

He turned in Natalie's direction, and she jumped,

knowing how it would look with her standing right there. She took a few steps forward and ended up bumping into him, not realizing he'd walked that quickly in her direction.

"Natalie, what are you doing here?" Easton's hands wrapped around her upper arms to keep her from falling backward. The grin on his face was something she realized she'd missed over the past forty-eight hours, and he looked like he missed her too.

She held up her stack of papers and said, "I got through all my chores this morning and realized I'd left all the papers I needed to grade here at the school."

Easton glanced down at his watch. "Well, I better not keep you. We only have a few hours until the carnival, and I want to go with you." His expression softened, and their gazes were locked for several seconds, causing Natalie's body temperature to rise significantly under his stare.

He leaned forward, and she wasn't sure what she'd do if he actually moved forward and kissed her, but there was no way she wanted to be caught kissing him with students coming in and out of the locker room.

When he wrapped his arms around her for a hug, Natalie was partly disappointed and partly relieved that she hadn't had to brush him off. It was going to be enough that they attended this evening together, and as much as she didn't want to think about it, she did prefer a first kiss with one of the most attractive and sensitive guys she'd ever met to be in a more intimate setting.

He pulled back and gave her a half-smile, teasing her with only a partial dimple. "I'll see you tonight." He said the words as though they were fact, and Natalie couldn't help but smile.

"I better get working on these, then." She waved to him, biting her lip as she turned around and moved toward her vehicle. The smell of him went with her, and she breathed it in, getting lost in thoughts of what the evening could bring.

How was it she'd started to fall for the one guy in Coldwater Creek who was technically off-limits for the Hirsch family?

She should probably stay home, make sure her father didn't fall back into his habit of drinking excessively and make sure she was caught up on grades and lesson plans. But the thought of being stuck at home was like being invited to a big party and then saying no.

No one in town knew her connection to the Hirsch name, and if she could keep it like that, things would continue to go smoothly. But if she wanted a long-term relationship to work, she'd have to tell Easton eventually. And as much as she wanted to believe that he'd understand why she hadn't been completely forthcoming, she still didn't know him that well just yet.

She picked up speed, now comfortable with the curves going up the short road to the house. She'd take the chance and go tonight. Maybe then she'd have a better handle on how to talk to both of the men in her life, the one who had fathered her, and the one who was rapidly taking up space in her heart.

$\mathcal{E}$aston paced back and forth in front of the diner. Natalie had texted an hour before that she would be there fifteen minutes ago, but there had been no sign of her since then. He'd been stopped by many of the older ladies in Coldwater Creek, asking him who or what he was waiting for, but he could see their minds working.

"A friend." Short and simple, giving them nothing else to gossip about.

Soon enough, he felt a tap on his shoulder and turned to find someone dressed as a witch, the face painted green and everything. He peered closer, trying to figure out who it was.

"It's me, Natalie. Why aren't you dressed up?" she asked, pulling some of her fake black hair out of her mouth.

"Um, we don't usually dress up for this. Did I tell you we did?" Panic coursed through him. He racked his brain, trying to remember every bit of conversation they'd had about the carnival.

She grinned, her bright white teeth contrasting against the dark green paint on the rest of her face. Shaking her head, she said, "No, I just thought it would spice things up. We can always help you get dressed up as well."

Not liking her tone, he looked at her out of the corner of his eye. "What do you mean?"

"Well, we can find something for you at the old thrift store a block away. I think it's still open for a few minutes. Want to try it?" She gazed up at him, her light blue eyes holding his attention and causing him to forget what they were talking about.

As the pieces all came together, he realized she wanted him to dress up, something he hadn't done since about the sixth grade. Not even for those dumb parties in college had he attempted to dress as anything but himself. He wasn't sure if it was a matter of pride or discomfort.

He waved his hand in the air and said, "I think we'll be okay. Let's just head over there."

"Come on. I think it'll be fun to dress up. Maybe we'll start a trend for next year." The pleading in her tone and on her face caused him to bite down, clipping the side of his tongue in the process.

"Fine," he said, walking in the direction of the thrift store. He'd wanted to spend time with this girl, but now his tongue hurt, and he was going to have to wear some weird costume that would probably make his skin itch.

Natalie caught up quickly, the long black dress swirling around her legs as she walked. Easton breathed out a long sigh. This was only for a couple of hours. He could handle anything for that long, and if it was something fun, maybe just pleasing her would help him enjoy it more.

"Why the witch costume?" he asked, glancing at her sideways.

"I've always loved witches. I'm actually the Wicked Witch of the West," she said, pulling up her skirt to reveal striped socks that looked just like the character from *The Wizard of*

Oz. From the side, he noticed for the first time that she'd done something to make her nose look a little more hooked than normal. "What do you usually dress up as?"

"Easton McBride."

"You don't even try to like this holiday?" She let her bottom lip jut out a bit in a pout.

Easton shook his head. "I like being in my regular clothes, so wearing a costume usually makes me feel uncomfortable."

"We'll keep it simple, then. Nothing over the top." She grinned at him again and pulled his arm in the direction of the door to the thrift shop.

Several aisles were set up with already-packaged costumes, and for each one Natalie pointed out, he prayed there wouldn't be one in his size. She moved on from there and started looking through several racks of clothing as Easton just wished he were anywhere but there.

After at least ten minutes of browsing, she turned to him, her hand to her mouth as she studied what he was wearing. Several seconds went by before her eyes grew wide and she jumped up and down a few times.

"I've got it! We're in the wrong store, though." She pulled on his arm, leading him out into the cool fall air. They walked down the sidewalk with Natalie always a step or two ahead.

"Can we just go to the festival? I really want some fried food." His tone sounded whiny, but part of him liked how determined she was.

"Oh, hush. You'll be fine, and you'll still be able to wear your clothes."

He frowned, not seeing what she was saying. "I will?"

She nodded and pulled him into the grocery store where she dragged him into the aisle of paper goods. When she stopped in front of the paper towels, he worried that she was somehow going to suggest they go toilet-papering.

Pulling a package of Brawny paper towels down from the shelf, she said, "Let's pay for this and go."

She handed the roll to him, and Easton looked down, everything clicking in just a few seconds.

"The Brawny guy, huh?" He grinned, smiling at her ingenuity. As he looked at the plaid shirt he was wearing, as well as the jeans with a belt holding them up, he realized he nearly matched the guy on the front of the packaging exactly.

"Yep. I figured if I pushed you too far outside your comfort zone, you wouldn't ever want to speak to me again." She laughed as they walked up to one of the self-checkout registers. She scanned it and took a small wallet out of the folds of her black costume, slipping a dollar bill and some coins into the machine.

"I'll admit, I was a bit worried at first, but seeing how much you like this, I figured I'd give it a chance."

She pulled the receipt from the machine and tapped it against his forearm. "If you think I like Halloween, just wait until you see me at Christmas."

With the beaming smile she gave him, Easton couldn't imagine what she would be like with all the other holidays, but he couldn't wait to find out.

Once they'd made it out to the sidewalk, they fell into step side by side. At one point, Easton reached out and caught her hand in his, trying to make it seem like the most natural thing in the world. He could see her smile out of the corner of his eye, but he was so focused on the energy flitting between their palms that he wasn't sure how his face looked.

They walked to the town square another two blocks down, where the area was abuzz with people going to and fro throughout the booths.

"This is amazing. They do this every year?" Natalie asked, readjusting her hat with her free hand.

Easton nodded. "Ever since I can remember. It's gotten a

lot bigger, more extravagant, over the past ten years. The woman in charge of it is into Halloween more than anyone else I know, so she makes sure everything is over the top."

"This is just right," Natalie said, looking up at him and squeezing his hand a bit. Emotions he'd not felt in years coursed through him. How was it that this girl he'd just met was causing all the walls he'd built about relationships to tumble faster than some of his linemen tackling the other team?

Whatever it was, he hoped it continued. Having someone to talk to and do stuff with was something he'd missed.

"Are you ready for some fried Oreos?" Easton asked.

"Lead the way," she said with a smile, melting any of the resentment he'd felt about dressing up. His feelings for this girl were getting out of hand and quickly, but for the first time in a long time, he didn't care.

CHAPTER 16

The carnival was so much fun, but Natalie could now feel every piece of sugar and fried food she'd eaten. They were walking back along the sidewalk in the direction of where she'd parked her car. With the dark sky above lit up with the bright stars, she sighed, feeling like she'd just accomplished something she'd never done before.

Easton had held her hand several times throughout the carnival, and each time he reached out for her, she thought her heart would explode with happiness.

As they drew near her car, Easton slowed down a bit, the look on his face a mixture of worry and fear.

"Why won't you let me come pick you up?" he asked, his words soft, his eyes turned up to the sky.

Natalie hadn't been expecting a question like that, and it took her a moment to process. In that time, Easton turned those big brown eyes in her direction, the pleading in them signaling that it was something that bothered him.

"I wasn't sure when I'd be done grading papers, and then I had a lot of things to buy today to get ready for Halloween on Monday. I just figured it would be easier than me driving home for you to pick me up, causing us to miss most of the carnival." She hoped her answer was satisfactory, and as she looked at him, he nodded after several seconds, as if that was the end of the conversation. "I'm pretty sure you live on the other side of the valley, too, so sometimes it's just easier to meet you."

"That's partly true." He turned to face her completely and placed his hands on her arms, looking down at her with a type of adoration she'd never experienced in her life. "Did you have a good time?"

She grinned. "I definitely did. I love that this town loves Halloween so much. Maybe you'll be more inclined to dress up next year. You had so many compliments—well, at least once people finally figured out who you were."

Easton chuckled, shaking his head slightly. "Yeah, who knew it would be that hard for people to get when you're pointing directly at the picture on the paper towels?"

"Please tell me there's something like this for Christmas."

"Bigger, if you can believe it." He smiled, the action warming her insides as she stared at him. How had she fallen for this guy so quickly? She'd always told herself she wouldn't really like someone until she'd known him for a while, but here she was, after a week or two, wishing that every night could be like tonight.

He moved forward an inch or two and looked like he was leaning in to kiss her, when a voice caused the two of them to jump.

"Coach McBride, I'm glad I finally caught up to you," an older man said, shuffling forward along the sidewalk. "You dropped your wallet next to the cotton candy booth a few minutes ago, and I wanted to make sure you got it back."

The man arrived next to them and looked from Easton to Natalie and back again. "Who's this witchy lady?" he said with a snort.

Easton and Natalie joined in, and she loved the sound of Easton's laugh, deep and hearty, like it was playing to her soul.

"Charlie, this is Miss—"

"I'm Natalie," she said, interrupting. She moved her hand forward and shook the man's hand, glad she'd decided not to color her hands green. She'd be lucky if she could get this off her face before school started on Monday.

"What's your last name, Miss Natalie? I don't believe I know you." He smiled, but there was something beneath his smile that implied she was some sort of outsider.

"Lynch, sir. I just started teaching at the school this year."

Waving his finger at her, the man said, "That's right. I remember one of my granddaughters saying she had a new English teacher this year. Well, we wish you good luck, especially once the winter comes. Not too many people stick around for the amount of snow we get here."

The man said goodbye to them and moved back in the direction of the carnival, leaving as abruptly as he came.

Natalie moved to pull out her car keys from one of her hidden pockets and jingled them in front of Easton. "I'd better get home before it gets any darker. Thanks again for a great evening."

Too nervous to see if he would try and kiss her again, even with the green paint, she walked around the car and got inside. Turning on the engine, she drove away, glancing back at Easton through her rearview mirror.

What she saw there wasn't just a football coach or a stuck-up athlete like she'd assumed on that first day meeting him, but a guy who was taking bits of her heart each time they met. It wouldn't be long before she'd have to make a decision, and she hoped she'd have the courage to tell her father she was falling for his enemy.

CHAPTER 17

The next two weeks seemed to speed by, and Easton kept in contact with Natalie as much as possible through texting. The postseason hadn't gone as he'd wanted, and his team ended up taking third place in the state, leaving a somewhat sour taste in his mouth. But Natalie had tried to cheer him up, helping him see that great things could happen next year and there was always another chance.

Want to do something tonight? he texted.

He stared at the screen as if she'd be responding right then. It had been so long since the carnival, but he wanted to see her again, needed to feel that same electricity flowing through him as happened each time they touched.

I can't tonight. Prepping for the play. You can always come help backstage if you want.

Easton's nose twitched up. He'd almost forgotten that was another of her teacherly duties. Plays weren't his thing. He'd always made fun of the kids who were in them when he was in high school, and while that probably wasn't the best thing, he wasn't exactly interested. But he'd actually had fun the night she'd dragged him around to find a costume. Maybe it wouldn't be as bad as he imagined.

Later that night, he drove into town, all his chores done at the ranch at a reasonable time now that football didn't occupy a large chunk of every day. He parked on the side that would be easier to access the drama area and walked into the building, rubbing his hands together to warm up somewhat. He'd seen on the weather report that they were due a large snowstorm that night, and he just hoped his truck would make it home through it. He'd put off changing his tires, and now he wished he'd listened to his mother about that.

As usual, his thoughts turned to Natalie, and he remembered her small car. How would it make it through? He would have to follow her home to make sure she arrived safely.

There were several students running through the halls, dressed in different costumes that seemed to be from the Shakespeare era.

"Hey, Coach," said one of the students in passing, while others looked like he had some plague growing on his face.

Moving backstage, he looked around for Natalie, wondering if he'd missed her in some other area of the auditorium.

"You made it. I didn't think I'd see you." She grinned at him and moved in for a hug, allowing him to breathe her cinnamon scent.

"I figured I'd come help you out. What do you need me to do?" He looked around, feeling more out of his element than he had in days.

She looked around and said, "How are you with a paintbrush?"

"Pretty awful, to tell you the truth. I think three-year-olds can paint better than I can."

Natalie bit her bottom lip, her hand raised as though

hiding that she was trying not to laugh. "Well, if you're willing, we could really use some help with finishing off our backdrops. Just tell Tina to give you the sections that don't have to be super detailed." She winked at him and flipped through what looked like a script in her hands. "I've got to get this rehearsal back on track. We start in three days, and I don't want them stumbling through everything."

She moved out into the hall and called the students back to the stage while Easton moved in the direction she'd pointed. Painting. He'd come in his nicest jeans and a crisp button-up shirt, hoping to spend some time with her. Decorating the décor for the background of a play was something he hadn't planned for.

But if he liked this girl, and if painting actually helped her to finish sooner, maybe he'd have a chance to take her for ice cream after.

"Are you Tina?" he asked a tall girl with a palette of colors in her hand.

She turned and smiled. "Yes. How can I help you, Coach?"

"I'm here to help. But I'm no artist, so whatever I can do to not mess up the overall look, that would be great." He rolled up his sleeves and found an apron slung across one of the chairs.

"Okay, let me get you over to this section, then." The girl put the palette and paintbrush down on a chair and motioned for him to follow.

Standing in front of a large piece of wood attached to two wheels, Tina motioned to a bucket of paint at the bottom of it. "If you'll just use that paint right there and paint this entire wall, that will help me. I have to get the details done over here, and then I can come make this look like a castle wall."

Bending, he opened the lid to the paint, seeing a dark

gray color inside. "So I just have to cover the wood with gray?"

When she nodded, he breathed a sigh of relief. At least he couldn't mess that up.

Tina moved away, and Easton worked to pour some of the paint into the tray, grateful for the roller and long pole to help get as high as possible. This was a large piece, and it would take him some time, but as he heard Natalie give directions to the students on the stage behind him, Easton smiled, grateful for this little bit of time where he could hear her working with the students.

The amount of patience she had with the one kid who kept messing up his lines showed Easton that he had a lot to work on. He wasn't a yeller all the time on the football field, but he'd learned to use it at certain times to get his players' attention or to help them get some motivation during a football game. But her constant assurance that the boy could and would remember the lines was something he wouldn't have been good at.

As the time passed, he realized how passionate she was about drama, and he chuckled softly. He'd never really pictured himself falling for a girl who'd be interested in all the opposite things he was, but maybe that was to help work him out of his comfort zones. He'd been doing the same things he'd done for years, and now that she'd come into his life, it seemed to give him different perspectives on what he'd thought was fact but was really just his opinion.

Over two hours and a sturdy ladder later, he'd finished painting the entire wall. It had been a rush near the end as the small bit of the perfectionist within him couldn't leave the top section unfinished. But then again, he didn't want to be stuck in the school with no one else, and it sounded as though most of the rehearsals were nearing their end.

He washed out the roller brush and made sure to put

everything where Tina directed. It felt different being bossed around by a seventeen-year-old girl, but he went with it, knowing it was easier than trying to guess.

Paint had spattered all over his forearms and hands. He was grateful for the apron he'd found, or else one of his favorite shirts might have been set aside for his ranch pile.

"Thank you for doing that. It saves me so much time when I don't have to do all the base work."

"Are you the only painter here?"

The girl rolled her eyes and shook her head. "No, but the other two are dating, so I never see them. If you want to come back on Monday night, I'm sure I could use your help again." She smiled at him, hopeful.

"I'll see what I have going on at the ranch and let you know." Easton waved goodbye and moved to find Natalie.

"You're still here?" she said in shock as she looked up from the stack of papers spread out on the chairs around her in the audience seating.

"Just finished painting the castle wall. Are you all done here?" He stuck his hands into his pockets as he skipped the last step and landed on the ground at the bottom of the stage steps.

"Just about," she said, sticking a pencil into her mouth as she picked up a pile of papers and leafed through them. "I need to make sure I mark where we need to rehearse again on Tuesday. I'm hoping Principal Jackson will let the kids out of their eighth-period class then. Otherwise, we won't be able to do the full run-through before our first show on Wednesday."

Easton stood in front of her, grinning at the focus on her face. It surprised him to see that, as he'd only ever seen it in athletes ready to strike. The fact that she could take something like a play so seriously struck a chord within him. He'd been so closed-minded to a lot of new things, but now that he hoped to continue their relationship, he realized how much he'd been missing out on.

She gathered up all the piles, finishing just as the stage lights turned off.

"Ice cream?" he asked.

"I'd love to. Is the Red Baron open this late?" Her brows drew together as she looked down at her phone. "I don't think we'll make it in time."

One of the few downfalls to living in their small town. The Red Baron was a drive-in restaurant that had that classic old feel to it, and they made the best peanut butter chocolate milkshakes he'd ever had. He remembered craving them when he was at college.

"Let's go to the store and buy some. We can eat in my truck."

"Perfect. Let me drop these off in my classroom, and I'll grab my coat."

Five minutes later, they were walking out to his truck. Natalie slipped into her coat, her jaw moving rapidly against the cold air. Easton opened the door for her and waited until she slipped in, not realizing how cold it was inside the cab until he got in on the driver's side. He turned the heat up to full blast and rubbed his hands together.

"Sorry, I should have come out and warmed it up for you," he said, giving her an apologetic smile.

"It's fine," she said, rubbing her hands together.

Easton pulled out of the parking lot, maneuvering onto the road in the direction of the grocery store in Afton. It was a smaller one, but at least they'd have ice cream.

"Probably not the best thing to be eating when it's so cold out," Natalie said, chuckling. "But I love ice cream, so I'll eat it in a blizzard."

"I wouldn't be surprised if we got snow in the next week. This is the longest we've gone without it for years." Easton paused a moment. "I guess it's not too much of a change from Utah, right?"

"The wind is a little more intense here, but I think I'll survive." She grinned at him, moving her hands in front of the air vents to warm them up.

After grabbing small pints of ice cream, Easton the Moose Tracks and Natalie the Double Chocolate Peanut Butter, they drove down to the park near the school.

"Sometimes it feels like I never leave this place," Natalie said.

She looked up at the lit building, and Easton tried to study her profile out of the corner of his eye. With her lips pinched together, he wondered what could be on her mind.

"Do you like it here in Coldwater Creek?" he ventured to ask. He felt an attraction to her, but if she was going to be like most of the other young people in this town, they were looking to move on, find a different place to live with more to do at night.

"I really do. I mean, there are some things I miss about Utah, but for the most part, this is a slower pace, which I can use in my life. And I love directing the plays for drama. I never got to do that at the last school I taught at because the director had been there for over twenty years. I guess I lucked out that the one here just retired."

Easton nodded. He didn't know much about the drama department of Coldwater Creek High, but he could imagine what it would be like if the teacher had been there for decades. His mother had always wanted her boys to get into cultured activities, hoping it would balance out the sports side of life between football and rodeo, but it didn't sink in for many of the McBride children. Except for Molly, who he hadn't seen at practice that night.

"I forget. What's Molly's part in the play?" Easton asked, placing a spoonful of ice cream onto his tongue.

"Molly McBride?" Her eyes widened, and Natalie tipped her head back and laughed. "I probably should have made that connection a lot sooner. She's the sidekick of the lead female. But she was out sick today. I'm just hoping she can get better before next week. She has a lovely solo that explains a lot about what the main characters are going through. It would be a shame to miss it."

Frowning, Easton asked, "Don't you have backups or something?"

Natalie nodded. "We do, but the other girl isn't as talented as your sister."

Easton leaned partly against the seat and the door, smiling at the thought. He'd usually turned his brain off when his family began talking about plays and musicals, but he felt a surge of pride that his sister was pretty good at something she loved.

"What about you, Easton? Are you happy here? No thoughts about moving on to another place?" She raised her eyebrows and tipped her head down a bit, making the question seem more mischievous than anything.

"I grew up here and then went to college somewhere else. I thought I'd made it when I was drafted by the Patriots, that all those hours I'd put in when I was so doggone tired after working on stuff around the ranch had finally paid off. And playing to a packed stadium. There's nothing like it."

He took a breath, letting the familiar emotions sweep over him like it was happening again. His mind put the first three games on a quick replay and then slowed way down for the hit that ruined his career. "I got injured in the fourth game and after all the X-rays and MRIs, the doctors told me I wasn't going to be playing football again. Coming back home was one of the hardest and best things for me."

"I didn't know you were a pro-football player. That's pretty cool." She grinned at him and he studied her face, trying to read how she felt about it. Was she one of the jersey chaser types? He didn't think she was but his senses about these kinds of things were usually way off.

He paused a moment, trying to line up his feelings with the correct explanation. "I guess I always knew at some point I was going to be a rancher. I just didn't think it would be so soon. And with my dad having a heart attack a few months ago, it's good that I'm here and learning all I need to from him."

"I'm so sorry about your father. Is he all right?"

"Yeah, he's fine. I think it just irks him that he's not the young buck he used to be. He could have had it worse, though. The father of one of our good family friends had a stroke and lost mobility on one side of his body."

Her eyebrows furrowed together, and she rolled her lips in as if she were seeing the pain firsthand. "That is awful. Do you enjoy ranching? Or are you worried something like that will happen to you later?" She flashed him a half-grin, her spoon poised over her ice cream as she awaited his answer.

"I haven't really thought about it in depth, but I'm happy when I'm with you. And coaching football gives me that taste of what I missed, but I still have the advantage of being with my family and not having to travel too much. And ranching, well, I think once I can officially take it over from my dad, I'll love it then."

"I can understand that. Sometimes we want to try out a different way but because it's been done a certain way for so long, there is some kickback from our parents."

Easton turned to look at her, curious. This was a detail she hadn't revealed yet. "What kind of business are you talking about?"

She rolled her lips in, her cheeks coloring a bit, and she looked down at the pint of ice cream as though trying to hide somewhat.

"I grew up around animals, and seeing the way my father does things can work. I just think there are other ways to connect to buyers. The internet and social media are a great way to reach out beyond locals, but he doesn't see that."

"Yes!" Easton said much louder than he'd intended, causing Natalie to jump. "Sorry, I mean, I feel like I've been trying to drive that point home to my father for months now. The hard part is getting the social media established enough to make a difference. I think we're finally getting to the point where he can see it as valuable and not a waste of my time."

"Sounds like we have way more in common than I thought."

Easton let a spoonful of his ice cream melt on his tongue, thinking over their conversation. "Why were you so hostile to me when you found out who I was?"

Natalie's eyes went wide, and she visibly swallowed. "Um, I'd just heard a few things about you and let those opinions rule without really getting to know you first."

He nodded. He could understand how that would work. But who would have been spreading rumors about him? Not that he was the special citizen of Coldwater Creek, but he did what he could to help others around the valley. He'd heard plenty of smack talk when he was playing in college and his short stint with the NFL, but he thought he'd gotten past that for the most part.

"Well, Natalie, what is one of your greatest wishes or dreams?"

She gave him a shy smile, her eyebrow raising as she stared at him. "I'd like to tell you, but then I don't think it would come true."

"I'll figure it out. Someway or somehow, I'll find out what it is." He smiled at her, his hand reaching over to cover hers on the seat next to him. That same eruption of tingles passed through his hand, up his arm and into the rest of his upper body.

She licked her lips, and for a moment, Easton was tempted to lean forward and capture them with his own. Instead, he glanced at the clock.

"I should probably take you home. I don't want to keep you out too late on a school night." He studied her face, wondering if she was feeling like this was more than a friendship.

"My car is at the school. Just drop me off there."

"Do you need me to follow you home? It looks like it's starting to snow." He pointed out the window.

Natalie shook her head. "I'll be fine. My car has made it through worse on the hills of Logan."

He drove the short drive to the school parking lot and put his truck into park. Before he could open his door to go open hers, she'd slid out of the truck with a wave and a thank you for the ice cream.

He drove home, his mind on their conversation, wondering if he'd been reading all the wrong signs. Had he been delegated to the friend zone?

For some reason, that thought hurt more than he wanted it to. He'd found himself waiting for her texts and wanting to know her opinion on most things. Thoughts of her were never far from his mind.

Maybe it was better if they were just friends. Then he wouldn't have to figure out a way to bail out and make things awkward like he always did. In such a small town, it wasn't like it was easy to hide from past dates or relationships. His last real girlfriend ended things between them the week before graduation from college, and while his mother had worked hard to set him up with every girl in the county once he'd arrived back in Coldwater Creek, it just seemed like it would never work.

Sometimes the excuse was he spent too much time on the ranch, moving cattle and doing chores, and not enough time with whoever it was at the time. It was the crutch he'd been using lately to not even try to get involved romantically with anyone, but there was a pull toward Natalie that made him want to give it a go.

But was that something she wanted? Only time would tell.

CHAPTER 18

*N*atalie readied herself for the opening performance of the fall play, running around backstage to make sure everything was taken care of. The girls who took care of makeup had finished with all the main actors several minutes before and only had to touch up a few for the ones who would show up in later scenes.

Costumes were on, and all the stage crew gave her a thumbs-up. This was it, the start of something she loved and hoped to continue for years at Coldwater Creek.

She made her way into the orchestra pit, settling in as she waited for the crowds to take their places and the show to begin. Her insides buzzed with anxiety and anticipation, but she knew her students would perform, that they knew their parts inside and out.

Her thoughts turned to Easton and his text earlier, something similar to texts she'd sent to him during football season.

Good luck tonight. Break a leg.

She hadn't had time to text him back, but it made her smile that he'd actually made an effort. Plays and musicals seemed to make him as uncomfortable as dressing up for Halloween, so she didn't expect to see him there. And since she was just directing, she didn't want to bore him by having him come and sit for two and a half hours while he waited for her.

But he seemed to always be in the back of her mind, the one safe person she could see herself with. She'd almost told him her silly childhood dream of dressing up in a fancy gown and dancing the night away. But a guy like him wouldn't understand something like that. He'd probably had his pick of girls for the high school dances.

She'd gone to plenty of dances throughout the years, but most of them were the "girls ask" or the fun "let's be friends" type of guy dances. None of them had allowed her the chance to pick out a beautiful gown and get all dolled up for a night of fun. She should've been over it by now, should've put that behind her after getting married, but since she and Craig had never had a first dance due to his inebriation that night, she still hadn't fulfilled that hope. Maybe that was why she loved helping the student council plan them now.

Easton had no plans to leave Coldwater Creek, and from everything she'd learned about him, he was an upstanding guy who wouldn't string her along if he didn't feel the same. That thought sent a thrill shooting up her spine, and she grinned, cueing the actors to begin.

The time passed faster than she'd anticipated, and with only a few minor blunders, they'd survived the first night of the performance. Natalie made it backstage, congratulating her students on their performances.

"Well done, Natalie," she heard her father say behind her. Turning, she found his eyes clear and a grin on his face. He'd even dressed up a bit, a plaid button-up along with his best jeans. His combed hair made her wonder if he was hoping to see more than just the play that evening. Had he met a woman who was helping him change? Because it certainly wasn't from her own efforts.

Wrapping her arms around her father, she said, "Thanks, Dad. I'm surprised you came. Wasn't the last time you came to one of these when I was in high school?"

"Sounds about right. But I figured I should probably come support you. After all, I don't have to drive several hours to do so."

Natalie glanced behind her father, her eyes widening when she saw Easton striding toward them. How was she going to maneuver this situation?

He stood a few feet behind her father, a beautiful bouquet of flowers in his hands. With a big grin, showing off that dimple, he said, "You did a great job, Natalie."

His voice caused her father to turn, his body going rigid at the sight of Easton standing there. "What do you want with my daughter?" Her father's tone was harsh, and Natalie cringed just hearing it.

Confusion covered Easton's face as he looked between the two of them and then stared at Natalie as if silently demanding her to deny it.

She nodded, turning her eyes to the ground, trying to steel herself from what was about to happen. All the happiness she'd felt from the end of the show had fizzled, and she just wished she could escape and somehow redo this night now that she knew Easton would be there.

"I just thought I'd bring her some flowers, sir," Easton said, a hard edge to his tone. The way he was looking at her father was probably matched, the narrowed eyes and hard jaw.

Natalie stepped between them, reaching out for the flowers. "They are beautiful." She held them up to her nose and smelled them. "Thank you for coming. I didn't think you'd make it."

"Is there something going on between you two?" Her father's words brought her back to the reality of the situation.

"No," she said, turning to look at her dad.

"Yes," Easton said at the same time.

Natalie turned back to look at Easton, but his expression looked more like a mask, shielding her from seeing his real feelings.

After staring at her for a few more seconds, Easton turned and stalked back down the hallway he'd come through.

Natalie turned to her father. "I'll be right back."

She ran after Easton as fast as her pencil skirt would allow her to. Once she caught up to him, she lightly touched his arm, to which he flinched.

"Please, Easton, I can explain. I—"

"You can explain what?" he said gruffly, the sound coming through clenched teeth.

Using her hands to emphasize her words, she said, "I should have told you who I was from the beginning, that I'm Darryl Hirsch's daughter. But I guess I was scared it would change how you saw me, and after a while, I didn't want you to push me away."

Easton kept walking, lengthening his strides and making it difficult for her to keep up. "You should have told me." His furrowed brow and tightly pressed lips caused her to stop in her tracks, even while he continued out the doors and into the night. "I deserved at least that much. I guess you didn't feel the same way I did."

Frozen, her brain tried to reconcile all that had happened in the past few minutes. His use of the past tense caused her stomach to constrict, a shortness of air to her lungs causing her breaths to come out in rapid spurts. The realization settled in as tears welled up. She'd been through this before, but not because of something she'd done. This time, it was her fault that the guy she'd fallen for had walked away.

Turning back, she brushed the tears away with her fingertips, not wanting to explain anything to some of the students who stared at her as she passed. Her father hadn't moved, looking as though he'd been turned into a statue, even wearing the same expression of disbelief.

"Him? Of all the people in the world, you've spent your time with him?" His anger had subsided to disappointment, one that hurt worse than all the outbursts he could have released on her. The only two men in her life, and she'd disappointed them both.

"I didn't mean to, Dad. He just helped me get my car started one day and invited me to hang out, as friends. Things just seemed to snowball from there."

Shaking his head, he turned the opposite direction, moving out of the school just as quickly as Easton had done. Only this time, she didn't follow. There was no point. She'd seen the look on both of their faces, and she realized she'd really screwed things up.

Grabbing the locket between her thumb and forefinger, she rubbed it, wishing her grandmother could appear and help set things right again. How was she supposed to live with the man she'd betrayed while working to gain forgiveness from the man she now nearly loved?

CHAPTER 19

He could have been okay with her being the daughter of Darryl Hirsch, but the fact that she'd lied about it...he couldn't figure out why she hadn't told him. Maybe because of all the history there. There was no doubt her father had filled her head with every bad thing about Easton, but since they'd been spending more time together, he thought her opinion of him had changed at least somewhat.

And her answer to her father's question about there being something between the two of them? That had sent knives slicing through his heart. He should have known she wouldn't feel the same about him. A girl who was willing to uproot herself and move to this small town and take on so many different duties at the school wouldn't be impressed with the few activities Easton had filled his life with. And now that he knew who her father was, he knew she had great responsibilities at home as well.

Easton sped down the highway, slamming the steering wheel every so often as he replayed the scene over and over again. But as he replayed the snippets of conversations they'd shared, he should have guessed it.

She'd talked about taking care of animals and at one point talked about seeing her father in the present tense. Why hadn't he insisted he pick her up? He could have saved himself the awkward encounter this evening.

But at least she'd been the one to mess things up and not him. That was the one bright spot to his track record of bad relationships usually ended by himself.

He pulled into the long drive that led to the ranch house. Seeing several lights on, he groaned, wishing he could just snap his fingers and be in his room without having to go through an interrogation of his night.

Opening the door and walking down the hall, he found half of his family curled up in their usual movie-watching positions on couches and bean bags.

"How was the play?" his mother asked. "How did Molly do?" Easton had taken her ticket to the opening night, probably knowing how much it would mean to Natalie to have him there. She'd be going with his father and the rest of the family the next night to see the production.

"She did really well. Don't tell her, but I was surprised at how much she's improved." He gave his mother a small smile, hoping she wouldn't see past it to the hurt in his eyes. He leaned down and gave her a quick kiss on the cheek. "I'm going to head to bed. Got to get an early start in the morning."

He moved away before she could say anything to keep him there, making it to the safety of his bedroom in a matter of a minute or so. Without removing his coat or his shoes, he leaned back and fell onto the bed, staring up at the plain white ceiling. For some reason, this breakup seemed different, as if it had left some physical wound behind.

Was it the betrayal of finding out she was the daughter of a man who hated him? Not that Easton liked Darryl much better after he'd tried to slander his name through town for the past three years, but Easton just wished he'd been given that bit of information before meeting her father face-to-face.

Setting his jaw, he let out a deep breath. He'd move on, do what he had to do to get the Christmas Ball over with, hopefully with little interaction with her, and then he'd be fine. Other than at school functions, the chances of them meeting around town were slim, and he hoped to keep it that way.

He would get Natalie Lynch, or Hirsch, out of his mind now and go back to living how he'd done for the past several years since being told he couldn't play football anymore. Compartmentalizing their relationship would be the easiest way to deal with it.

CHAPTER 20

Finishing out the week of the play was more painful than Natalie could've imagined. Even despite the large amounts of snow that had fallen on the valley, the crowds were still filling up the auditorium, and she searched the rows each night for signs of Easton, hoping he'd come back so she could ask forgiveness. Seeing his sister perform only made things worse, as if grinding dirt into an open wound.

She'd called a few times, hoping he'd pick up and that deep, comforting voice would tell her it was all a bad dream. And then she'd sleep, her brain conjuring up what life would have been like had she told him from the beginning that she was Darryl Hirsch's daughter. The dream would go along happily until some invisible force would crush her car or smash through the house, causing her to sit up straight in a cold sweat, her heart racing.

Her father would barely speak to her, and it was the night before Thanksgiving when she found him with a bottle in his hand, sitting in his favorite recliner as he watched a football game.

"Dad, you don't need to drink. Easton—"

"Don't use that name in this house!" he barked, his eyes looking like steel boring into her.

"He doesn't like me anyway, so don't you worry about that. I never would have betrayed you on purpose, Dad. Sometimes, you can't choose who you fall for."

He bit on the side of his cheek, mulling her words over. "I can understand that much. That's how your mother and I got together."

Her breathing paused, surprised by this turn of conversation. She'd never really heard how her parents met or what had ended up causing them to drift apart. Natalie had always just assumed it was the alcohol.

"But that's still no excuse for liking the guy who shamed me in front of the rest of the town. He ruined my reputation, and now this is how we live." He looked up at the crack in the ceiling, waving his hands around at all the disrepair of the home.

Moving her jaw back and forth, Natalie debated whether or not to retaliate. Before she'd completely made up her mind, the words poured out of her. "I'd say you shamed yourself, Dad. People have always known you to be one of the town drunks. The way to prove them wrong is by giving it up, turning your life around, and getting back to training those horses full time. I got someone to agree to bring their horses after this long weekend. I just hope we can prove that I wasn't just filling them with hot air."

She stood, unable to continue sitting in the sweltering room. Walking out to the porch, she breathed in the crisp, chilly weather. As she rocked, she rubbed at her arms, wishing she'd brought out a blanket.

Reflecting over the past several days, she let the hot tears fall down her cheeks, sobbing at all the emotions churning through her. Other people made it so easy, getting together for a relationship and staying together thirty-plus years. Maybe that just wasn't in her genes.

Or maybe she didn't deserve a happily ever after. The world had looked dark since her grandmother's death, and as the anniversary approached, Natalie hoped she would be able to make it through. Here she was, in a town where she still knew next to no one and the only real friend she had was Melody, but even they didn't know everything about one another.

She cried until she had nothing left inside her, numb to the elements. For once, it would be nice to get what she actually wanted. But who else did she have to blame but herself? If she'd been upfront about everything, she could have avoided this whole mess in the process. But would she have gotten to know Easton the way she did now?

CHAPTER 21

Easton had trudged out early Thanksgiving morning to work on a fence with Walker, grateful for the earliness of it so he didn't have to talk as much. He'd been miserable ever since the play, but he'd done his best to cover it up around his family.

The McBride boys met to shoot clay pigeons for their annual tradition, and it did nothing to brighten his mood. Even dinner with his mother's cooking couldn't help him have a genuine smile.

"What's up with you lately?" Walker asked as they went out to gather some more firewood for the stove.

"Just trying to get everything situated for the winter. The snowstorm predicted for tonight has me going through my list of to-dos, and we still have some cattle up on the other range that we need to bring back." He shivered just thinking of the long days they would spend bringing the cattle down in the deep snow, most likely double the amount up in the hilltops as down in the valley.

Walker frowned. "That's a minor problem, and we've dealt with that in years past. What happened with Natalie? I haven't seen or heard about the two of you together in at least two weeks, and that's coming from some of the town gossips." He smirked and punched Easton in the shoulder.

Easton blew out a breath, trying to decide if he should say something or not. Walker was good about keeping secrets, and talking about it all might help.

"Turns out she's Darryl Hirsch's daughter."

Walker's eyes grew wide like gumballs, and he clapped his hand over his mouth. "Are you serious? Wow, that must have been quite a shock. How did you find out?"

"I went to opening night of the play, brought her some flowers and everything, which you know is out of my comfort zone. Her father was standing there and made the connection. Who was I kidding, thinking things could actually work out?"

"Well, you're usually the one who's breaking things off, so it sounds like you did so again, right?" Walker asked, his arms folded against his chest as he leaned on the side of the house. "Nothing's really different than most of your past relationships."

Easton frowned. "What are you talking about? She basically broke up our relationship for me. How am I supposed to date someone who lied to me about who she was this whole time? And I'm sure family gatherings would be as cold as the stream outside your lodge right now."

"Did she live here when you fired her father? From everything I remember about their family, she left when we were still in grade school, after her parents' divorce. She probably had no connection to it at all."

Pointing his finger in Walker's direction, Easton said, "You didn't see how guilty she looked when I found out. How she begged for me to let her explain."

"And did you?"

Biting his bottom lip, Easton replayed the events of that

night. He hadn't really given her that chance, but he'd been too keyed up to think straight.

"No. I left. Drove home."

"Maybe she could use an apology from you as well."

The door creaked open, and their mother's head popped around the doorframe. "Did y'all get lost?"

"No, Mom. We're coming," Walker answered, gathering up a load of wood. Once she disappeared, he turned and said, "I'm no expert on girls, but it might be good if you give her another chance, or at least let her talk it out with you. Sounds like you felt something for her. That's a start."

Before Easton could respond, Walker stepped into the house. Easton didn't want anyone else in the family to question him, especially his mother, who he was surprised hadn't said anything to him so far. There were a lot of things he loved about his mother, but the fact that she wasn't pushing on this issue made him grateful.

He'd had no chance run-ins with Natalie since that night, and he hoped to avoid any for a while, at least until he'd figured out what he wanted.

CHAPTER 22

"Okay, so we have plans for all the decorations and the music, as well as the food," Natalie said, looking around at the student council sitting in her room the first week of December. "Is there anything else we're missing for the Christmas Ball?"

Sarah raised her hand and asked, "What about the venue? Is it almost finished?"

Natalie gulped, having almost forgotten that the place where they were supposed to hold the ball wasn't completely finished. Thinking about the lodge only dredged up memories of Easton, and she did her best to shake those away.

Turning to Talon, she asked, "Will you ask your coach how things are going with that?" The best way to get over him was to pretend he didn't exist anymore. Or at least hope she didn't have to interact with him.

She had more important things to worry about in the coming week.

"Sure. He's been moving cattle, but he should be back soon."

The words seemed to ping off her heart, and she knew

that no matter how hard she tried, she was still going to miss their talks and miss all the time they'd shared together.

She let the students discuss the rest of the dance while she half listened, wishing for the millionth time that she could go back and change things.

When the bell rang, she sat at her desk in a daze, not feeling like doing anything.

"Knock, knock," came a voice from the door. Melody peeked in and waved, but Natalie barely saw her. "How are things going today?"

"I'm here. I'd say that's something." Natalie's voice sounded lower than normal.

"Well, what can we do to cheer you up? Why don't we head out and have a girls' night?"

Shaking her head, Natalie said, "I'm not in the mood to be out."

Melody sat on the corner of Natalie's desk, looking down with a sad smile. "Girl, it's been three weeks. You can't live like this forever. People are starting to talk."

"What people?" Natalie asked, that bit of information being the first interesting thing that had happened all day.

"Well, from what I've heard, the students have noticed you've been a little out of it. What can we do to help you cheer up?"

Crossing her arms on the desk, Natalie dropped her head on top of them, groaning. She'd thought she'd been doing a good job of acting like her normal self while in class.

"Rewind time and tell my younger self to grow some courage and tell Easton who my dad was from the beginning."

"Have you tried calling him?"

"I did the first week, but he didn't take any of them." She looked up, feeling hopeless.

Melody's eyebrows rose. "That's it? The guy you're in love with, and you tried to call him a couple of times?"

Sitting up, Natalie waved her finger a few inches from Melody's face. "I never said I was in love with him."

"Well, you're acting like it. Did you act like this after you told your husband you wanted a divorce?"

Natalie shrunk back and scowled. Melody's question dug deep, but as Natalie reflected on those memories, she realized that even then, she hadn't been as heartbroken as she was right now.

"But how do I get him to talk to me?"

"You know where he lives. Just go over and say you won't leave until he talks to you."

Natalie's stomach clenched. "He lives with his family. What if they're there at the time?"

"Natalie, dear, if you love the guy as much as I think you do, you're going to do whatever you can to get over this awful feeling, right? Who cares what his family thinks? If you show how much you love him, I'm sure they'll back you up."

Melody stood and walked to the door. "I've got to run, but call me if you need moral support." She disappeared, leaving Natalie to her thoughts.

Could she just go up and tell Easton she was in love with him? The thought made her chest burn, and she'd never felt something more right. It was a chance she'd be willing to take. Things had gotten better in her relationship with her father, and now that he'd been dating a gal from the town to the north, he was a little more open to certain things. She just hoped he wouldn't completely disown her when she told him she loved Easton McBride.

The thought sent another thrill through her. How was it possible she'd fallen for him so fast? With Craig, they'd dated in college, and she hadn't even said those three words until they'd graduated. Even then, did she feel like this? She couldn't quite remember.

Grabbing her coat and purse, she marched out to her car, ready to get over this feeling and hopefully be able to move on, no matter how he felt about it after.

CHAPTER 23

*E*aston was grateful to see the outskirts of the ranch. The deep snow from Thanksgiving had made it difficult to navigate the cattle through, but with the family's dog and plenty of help, they'd been able to make it this far from the other grazing ground.

A horse came up next to him, and Easton turned to see his father. "Well done, son. We made it this far."

"It was with the help of everyone, Dad."

His father grinned and nudged his horse forward, making large tracks in the snow. Easton followed suit, making sure every last cow was pulled into the large fence that lined the McBride property.

Easton wasn't as excited to unsaddle his horse and brush him down, but the animal deserved it after all they'd gone through in the past few days.

"Easton!" Molly's voice caused him to look up while the others continued brushing and feeding their horses.

"Hey, Molly! How's it going?" Easton lifted the large saddle from Stormy's back, resting it on the saddle rack at the side of the stables.

His sister was only a few inches shorter than him, but she bounded up and stood close. "Miss Lynch is here." Her voice was a whisper, but the mischievous grin gave away her thoughts.

Trying to sound calmer than he felt, he asked, "Why? What does she want?"

"She asked to speak to you. I'm not sure what about, even though I've tried to pry it out of her." Molly bounced on her toes as if this displeasure he felt was some kind of entertainment.

After bringing over a bucket of oats, he brushed through the snarls in his horse's mane. "How long has she been here?"

"About an hour. Mom said you could give her a call when you got back, but she insisted she wait." Reaching out, she rested her hand on the brush Easton was holding. "Let me do this for you. Best not to keep her waiting any longer than she already has."

Easton looked at Molly as though she'd been taken with a fever or something. It was so odd for his youngest sibling to worry about anyone but herself that this small token of kindness caused him to wonder what was up. He'd hoped to have a few minutes to reason over how he felt before he faced Natalie.

Conceding the brush, he stomped through the snow and into the mudroom, taking his time to pull off his thick winter coat and all the other layers he'd worn underneath it.

Walking out into the kitchen, he got himself a glass of water, drinking deeply from the cool spring water that flowed through the faucet. When he turned around, he jumped slightly, seeing Natalie there staring at him.

She was still just as beautiful as ever, her bright red lips contrasting the light skin of her cheeks. Her blonde hair had been pulled back in a ponytail, but it was her eyes that drew him. There was a sense of sadness there, and from the slight dark circles he saw underneath them, he knew she hadn't gotten much sleep for who knew how long.

"Easton, I'm sorry to have barged in on you like this," she began, twisting her scarf between her hands. "I just needed to say I'm so sorry—"

He raised his finger and set it against his lips, hearing footsteps coming from the mudroom. He didn't want his whole family hearing this conversation, no matter how it turned out.

She stopped, her mouth clamping shut like she'd just been slapped across the face. He walked past her, waving at the last moment for her to follow him out to the back porch. It was out of range of the mudroom, and they hopefully wouldn't be disturbed. As he saw the pile of logs, it reminded him of his brother's conversation with him on the day of Thanksgiving. Walker had started dating Lauren Burke since then.

He turned to face her, leaning up against the tall stack of chopped wood. "Why are you really here?" His tone was colder than he'd meant it, but all the frustration that had built up over the past few weeks every time he thought about her betrayal seemed to be surfacing, making it difficult to hide.

She took a breath, her eyes on the ground for several seconds before the crystal-blue gems moved to his own. "I'm really sorry. It was selfish for me to keep something like who my father was a secret, given your history." She paused, looking into his eyes for something that he hadn't quite figured out yet. "To be honest, I only know the one side. And I'm sorry for assuming things at the beginning, but as we spent more time together, I got to the point where I just wanted to be with you."

Easton narrowed his eyes, trying to decide if she was

telling the truth. Walker's words drifted back to him as if it were only minutes ago. *She wasn't here when it happened.*

Was she asking him for his side of the story? The thought made him pause. But he shook it off. How could he trust her now? Sure, his friends and family had joked about him only wanting to have success in everything he did, which made him leave a relationship before it could blow up. But this time, he knew that if he gave in, he'd be vulnerable for another letdown, and after all he'd suffered in his life, he didn't think he'd survive it and be the same man as before.

"You could have tried to let me know who you were. After all the little things, don't you think you could have trusted me to open up about the situation?"

Her gaze flicked to the ground for a second before she looked back up, moisture in her eyes. "Believe me, I would have had I known I would start to lo-like you. But knowing how my father feels about you made me second-guess myself. And then I kept telling myself I'd tell you the next time we talked, which turned into the next, until I kind of forgot about it."

"Forgot about telling me who you are related to?" He closed his eyes, trying to rein in the anger surging. "If you really want to know what happened, your father showed up to the pregame of one of the football games hammered. When I told him to go home and sleep it off, he started throwing chairs and emptied out the water jug all over our starting offensive line."

He paused, feeling the adrenaline surge as if the memory was happening in real life all over again. Taking a breath, he focused on Natalie, working to change his tone. "I caught his arms and did my best to carry him out to the parking lot. One of the other coaches had dialed the police department, and I set him in the back of my truck to cool off."

"That was it? He made it sound like you'd run his name through the mud after."

Raising his hands, Easton took a step back. "I haven't said anything about it other than the statement that the authorities were required to take from me. My family knows, but they're the only ones. If anyone's name has been through the mud, it's mine because of what he's said to try to sway people to get me fired."

Natalie's face showed her understanding, and her shoulders rolled in, looking more resigned than he'd ever seen her.

"Thank you," she said, her voice just louder than a whisper. "I needed to hear the other side, and from my father's track record of drinking, I'm sure you've got a clearer picture of what happened than he does. I'm going to head home, but thank you for hearing me out. Again, I'm sorry I didn't say anything, and thank you for everything you've done for me." She gave him a close-lipped smile and stepped off the porch, wading through the deep snow around the side of the house.

"You can go through the front," Easton called out, watching her walk away as if she carried the world on her shoulders.

She turned and shook her head. Giving him that same smile, she disappeared around the corner. Taking a few moments, Easton tried to gather his thoughts. She hadn't been mad about what had happened with her father and was even more understanding about it all than he'd expected.

A pit formed in his stomach, releasing feelings of guilt and frustration. He shouldn't have been so hard on her. She probably had it worse than he did, having to put up with her father day in and day out.

But his real question now was, did she apologize because she felt guilty about everything that had come between them? Or because she hoped they could mend things and go back to the way they had been?

Easton worked through the conversation again, memorizing every expression on her face. She'd shown so much sorrow. He couldn't imagine what she'd been feeling. And she'd apologized for not telling him sooner.

He heard her car start and pull away, the familiar squeal of the engine as it shifted gears striking a chord within him.

The door creaked open, and Molly came out and sat next to him on the windowsill. "How'd it go?" Her expression was surprisingly serious. Something he hadn't seen from his sister in quite a while.

"Not good. And now I feel horrible."

"Well, there's no time like the present to make up for it. Go tell her how you feel."

Easton frowned, trying to figure out what his sister was getting at. "What do you mean, how I feel? I'm annoyed and frustrated and—"

"In like, or maybe even in love," Molly said with a smirk.

"I am not in love with Natalie Hirsch or Lynch or whatever her name is. I would know if I was in love with her." He set his jaw and stared out into the white expanse before them.

Molly scoffed. "Please, you've been a bear ever since you found out about her father. And she's been pretty miserable too."

"How did you know that's what happened? And what do you mean she's been miserable?" The curiosity perked up in Easton, and he waited for his sister's response.

She raised one eyebrow and shook her head. "You're so daft. The whole scene with you and her father and Natalie happened with half of the cast coming in and out of the backstage area. My friends told me all about how you brought her flowers and then freaked when you found out Mr. Hirsch is her father."

Easton closed his eyes and leaned his head back against

the glass. Of course, all the students knew what had happened. He was surprised he hadn't heard anything from the adults since that incident, but most people knew to leave him alone when it came to relationships.

"And what about her having a hard time?"

"She's not the same upbeat teacher I had before this whole thing happened. And I can probably peg when you two started hanging out because she was practically humming all the time. She's got a thing for you, Mr. Hotshot McBride. So don't go screwing this one up." Molly jabbed him with her pointer finger, grinning at him.

Shaking his head, Easton mulled over her words, wondering if she really did have feelings for him. "Tell Mom I'll be in in a minute. I need to go for a walk."

Molly leaned in and gave him a hug. "You've got this, East. Now, figure out what you want and make it right."

He chuckled a moment. It was the first time he'd done that in some time, and the feeling was refreshing, pulling him out of his funk for a few minutes.

He grabbed his boots from the mudroom and pulled on his jacket, grateful he didn't see anyone else in his family at the time. Striding toward the thick forest of pine trees on the slopes of the property next to a large mountain, Easton did his best to go over his feelings.

It had been some time since he'd actually been attracted to a woman, and every time he'd seen Natalie, he'd definitely wanted to spend more time with her. But there was also the ease of communication, which he'd never found with anyone else, especially none of the single ladies in Coldwater Creek.

But the drawback was that if he went for her, told her how he felt, would he be the loser? He'd made a promise to himself that he would do everything he could to win in his life after his career-ending injury, and sadly, that promise had done more detriment than good to his personal relationships in the past, making him feel like he'd come in last place in that part of his life.

He was in the red zone, and there were only two options: go for the touchdown or give up and punt to the other team. Could he stand to lose Natalie? That was something he needed to figure out.

CHAPTER 24

Natalie had driven away from the McBride house with a dry face, something she hadn't expected after Easton's tone toward her. But the fact that she'd learned his side of the story about her father being fired helped to ease some of the pain. Now she just needed to push forward, get the Christmas Ball over with, and focus on getting her father's business back on track.

His new relationship with Diane Withers was doing wonders for his transformation, and seeing them together made her miss those small moments with Easton. The way he'd caught her when she was about to trip at dinner at the lodge and how that dimple made her knees go weak every time she thought about it.

No matter how much she tried to push Easton out of her mind, he seemed to stick even more, like he'd been put there with glue or adhesive tape. She'd messed things up and had done everything she could to apologize for it. If he felt anything for her, it was his turn to show her.

Walking in the door to her father's home, the air smelled

of cooked meat and veggies. Diane stood behind the stove, shifting things around in a large pan with a wooden spoon. Natalie's father looked like he was grating cheese. It was a shock to see him helping out in the kitchen, something he'd never done growing up when she and her mother had lived there or even since she'd moved back home.

"Hello," Natalie said, unwrapping the scarf from around her neck. She was grateful she'd had it. It wasn't until she'd walked inside the heated home that she'd realized how numb she'd been on the way home.

"Hi, Natalie," Diane said, a genuine smile on her face. "We're just making some chicken fajitas for dinner. Have you eaten yet?"

Natalie shook her head and smiled. "Can I help with anything?"

"I think we're about ready," her father said, a small smile on his face. It was the first small concession on his vendetta to be angry with her, and she accepted it as a gift. "Just a minute," he said. "I want to see what the score is of the football game."

Natalie sat at the table, and an awkward silence took over the kitchen in his absence. Natalie liked Diane, but they'd never really had a one-on-one conversation. "Long day at school?" the woman asked, turning toward her.

Natalie nodded. "Yes and no. I went to apologize to someone for omitting certain details, and now I don't know how to feel."

"Easton McBride?" The look on the woman's face was sympathetic, but the fact that she'd come to that conclusion unnerved Natalie.

"Yes. I think I love him, but there's no shot there. It's almost like I'm numb and I'll realize just how much it will hurt later."

Diane turned off the burner and walked over to sit at the

table. "Never say never, Natalie. I've always had a thing for your father. I'd see him at events here and there and wonder about him. But things will happen when the time is right. For some of us, it just doesn't line up as soon as we want it to."

"You've liked my dad for a while? When did you start dating?"

"Just a few weeks ago. He came barreling down the sidewalk on his way to one of the bars and ended up running into me with a big bag of things I'd bought at that craft store right next to it. He apologized and helped me pick everything up. We started talking and ended up standing by our cars for a few hours, until it was too cold. I gave him my number, and we've been doing things together since."

Natalie wondered if it had been the night after the play. She was just grateful that someone else was watching out for her father, helping him change where she couldn't.

A hard lump formed in her throat as she thought about all the little things she'd done with Easton. He'd been there when her car broke down and had taken her out for ice cream even when the weather had turned cold. Nothing was overly grand, but it was all the bits of perfect she could have imagined when she fell in love.

She stared at Diane and smiled. Reaching her hand across the table, she grasped the older woman's hand and said, "Thank you for that."

"He's been sober since the high school play he came to see you at. I guess not knowing what was going on in your life because of his addiction made him realize how much time he'd lost with you. And he's quite a different man now, much like the one I remembered from when you and your mother lived here."

It was almost like her grandmother had sent this woman to tell her the things she couldn't.

It would only be a few more days until the anniversary of

her grandmother's death, but for some reason, she didn't feel like the world was coming to an end because of it. Maybe having some support behind her would help with that.

CHAPTER 25

*E*aston wasn't sure what it was, but ever since he'd talked to Natalie, he'd continued to analyze their conversation, finding the grace that had come with her actions. She'd apologized, stated her feelings for him simply, and hadn't thrown a huge tantrum while walking away. That was unlike any of the other girls he'd taken on just one date.

To top it off, as he thought more about it, many people had walked out of her life. Had she grown accustomed to it? Or was that just something she'd worked through to accept?

It was the day before the Christmas Ball, and he'd just helped Walker and Lauren, Walker's new girlfriend, put up the Christmas tree and finalize everything in the large ballroom. But he hadn't seen Natalie anywhere during the preparations.

Pulling aside one of the student council members, he asked if she'd seen her.

The girl shook her head. "No, she wasn't at school today either. I think it's some kind of big anniversary for her."

Easton thanked her and did his best to try and remember

what kind of anniversary it could be. The one from when she got divorced? Or when her mother remarried?

"What's eating you?" Walker asked, dropping another box of white twinkle lights that needed to be hung along the walls with the tulle.

"I just need to talk to Natalie, but that girl over there said she took the day off for some anniversary. I can't remember what anniversary she's talking about." He'd gone through their meetings with a fine-toothed comb, trying to remember.

Lauren walked up to Walker and Easton, a frown changing her features a bit. "Natalie Lynch? Yeah, I've talked to her a few times over the last few weeks. She was preparing for the anniversary of her grandmother's death, I think. I know they were pretty close, and it was hard for Natalie."

Walker and Easton turned to look at Lauren, both with their mouths dropped open. "You've been back in town for maybe a month, and you're already friends with her?" Easton's words sounded lame to his own ears. But he knew how private Natalie could be. Maybe she'd talked to her because Natalie and Lauren were some of the few younger women in town, or the fact that Lauren talked to just about everyone could have been a factor.

"Yeah, I've seen her a lot at the grocery store. We chat a bit, and she mentioned this was coming up."

Walker turned to Easton. "If you love her, you'd better go find her. She might need you today." Looking around at the room, he said, "Lauren will make sure we've got this place all spruced up for the dance."

Easton gave him a grateful smile and ran out of the room, wrapping his coat around him as he flew out the door. He drove as fast as the snowy roads would let him, maneuvering through Afton and then up the small canyon where he knew the Hirschs lived. Once he'd parked in the driveway, he bounded up to the door, pounding on it with his fist.

Over a minute passed before the door opened to her father standing there with a frown on his face. "What are you doing here?"

Easton did his best to look past the man and into the house. "Is Natalie here? I need to speak to her."

"She's not here, and if she were, I'd probably say the same thing." The man's lips tightened into a thin line.

Easton took a breath, realizing he needed to fix this situation first.

"Darryl, I know there have been a lot of things that have come between us, but I just want to say I'm sorry. I didn't want you to get fired because you're one of the best defensive line coaches I've been around. Your coaching made it so my days as quarterback at Coldwater Creek were a lot easier, with the defense stopping everyone and allowing me to guide the offense to score points. I'm sorry everything turned out the way it did, but the district took over, not me. I know you've had your troubles, but when you're sober, you're a pretty great guy." Easton watched as the hard lines on the man's face eased up, the tension in his shoulders causing him to relax.

Darryl started to smile but then cocked his head to the side. "You're not just saying that so you can see my daughter, are you?"

Easton shook his head. "No, sir. I learned quite a bit from you in the time we coached together, and I know the boys did as well. I've always been a bit prideful, but to be honest, coaching football is all about teamwork among coaches. We've had some good years, but our defense hasn't been as good as it could be."

A large smile appeared on Darryl's face, lighting up his face and reminding Easton of Natalie. After a few seconds,

Darryl sobered and glanced away. When he looked back, he said, "I'm sorry too. I shouldn't have gone around telling stories of a night I couldn't even remember. I just figured you got whatever you wanted and that was the only way I could really hurt you at the time."

Darryl reached out his hand, and Easton shook it, grateful to have one less thing between them. As if reading Easton's inner thoughts, Darryl said, "She went to Logan, Utah. She told me she'd be back tomorrow morning before the ball."

"Is she okay? Will she be okay?"

"My daughter's a strong one, but I think it took her a while to figure that out. But I know that if you're here to see her, that would mean more than any comfort I could give."

Easton shifted his weight to the other foot, trying to puzzle his feelings together. "Well, sir. I really like your daughter, and I hope to make up for all the dumb things I've done in the past few weeks when she gets back."

"What did you have in mind for asking forgiveness?" Darryl asked.

"I'm open for any ideas you have."

Motioning inside, Darryl grinned. "Come in. Let's chat."

CHAPTER 26

Natalie got an early start for Wyoming, hoping to make it back in plenty of time to inspect the lodge and make sure everything was in place. Principal Jackson hadn't been thrilled when she'd asked for yesterday off, but after explaining that she really needed this, he understood.

Her time in Logan had been healing and enlightening. Over the past year, she'd worried about how she would tackle each of the bigger events in her life without her grandmother by her side, but as she knelt before the grave, she realized her grandmother had been there in some ways, just like when Diane had given her a few bits of wisdom.

She'd received a text from Easton yesterday while she was there, and that sliver of hope she'd kept about them being together was now a flicker.

I hope you're okay today. I didn't know today was the anniversary. Just know you're in my thoughts.

It wasn't anything romantic, but at least he'd made contact. That was enough to help boost her throughout the evening.

The roads were slushy, but since there was no ice and she had her winter tires on her car, she took things slow and made it to her father's home around noon.

"Hey, Dad. I'm back." She shut the door behind her and walked into the house, trying to find him.

Her father came out of the back room and shut the door, a guilty expression on his face.

"I'm glad you made it back safely. A girl named Lauren stopped by last night with several items she said you'd need for tonight." He waved to the bathroom in the hall, and Natalie took in a deep breath as she saw several dresses hung up along the shower curtain rod. A few bags of makeup were sitting on the small edge of the sink, as well as a couple of curling irons.

"Did she say what I was supposed to do with all this?"

"She said to call her when you got back and she'd come get you ready for tonight." Her father smiled and pulled her into a side hug. "Sounds like you're starting to make some good friends here, dear."

Tears welled up in her eyes. She'd talked to Lauren a few times in the past few weeks, and she already felt as close or even closer with her than she did with Melody, making her feel a bit more at home.

"Okay, well, I'm going to head over to Silver Brook Lodge. I'm sure Principal Jackson is panicking that I haven't been there yet to make sure everything is in place." She walked back to the door, wondering if she could handle the fifteen-minute drive after sitting in the car most of the morning.

Her father stepped in front of her, the brace on his foot clomping on the hardwood floor. "I'm pretty sure they've got everything taken care of. Why don't you come rest until Lauren gets here? I've already taken care of the horses today and started up a little training." He beamed like he was the child waiting for a compliment from his mother.

"I don't know what's gotten into you, but all these changes look good on you, Dad. Could Diane be the reason for some of it?"

He nodded and then said, "And you. I didn't like it much when you first got here, ruining the groove I'd mastered since you and your mother left here, but it was the changes you suggested that helped me finally see Diane as someone I could love." He paused and visibly swallowed, his eyes filling up with tears. "And I'm sorry for everything in the past, for making things difficult for you and for trying to poison you against Easton. I think he's a better guy than I gave him credit for."

Natalie stared at him, wondering if she'd just dreamed he'd said those words. "Did I just hear you say better guy and Easton in the same sentence?"

Her father laughed, the sound long and deep like when she was younger. "I know; I'll have to eat a lot of the words from the past, but if that's who you love, then I'll not stand between you two." He reached up, brushing her cheek with his thumb before pulling her into a hug.

She had to be dreaming. This would never happen in normal life. She pinched her arm, feeling the full effect of it. He pulled back, and she gave him a small smile, still unsure what to think of the past several minutes.

"I should really go check on the lodge," Natalie said, trying to edge past her father again. But the door opened at that moment, causing her to jump back in surprise as Lauren came through the door.

"I just came from there, and it's looking fabulous. Principal Jackson will definitely approve." She grinned at Natalie and then at her father. "I know I said to call, but it's getting late and I wanted to have enough time to get you ready, so I just drove up. Are you ready to get all dolled up? We can't have the organizer of the ball going in jeans and a sweatshirt."

Natalie couldn't move, stunned by whatever this had turned out to be. Lauren led her in the direction of the bathroom. Pulling the dresses from the curtain rod, she moved them into one of the bedrooms down the hall.

"Go ahead and take a shower, and we'll go from there. I brought a bunch of dresses because I wasn't exactly sure what size you are, but I'm sure we'll find one that fits."

"Why are you doing this?" Natalie finally managed, her mouth catching up with at least one of the questions spinning in her brain.

Lauren grinned. "Because I love helping people get ready, and because that doesn't happen too often in this town." She pushed Natalie into the bathroom and closed the door.

The thought of dressing up for the ball was exhilarating, and she finally got moving. She just hoped Easton would be there and that she could finally tell him the whole truth about how she felt for him.

CHAPTER 27

*E*aston had been working since early that morning on several of the ranch chores, as well as a special surprise for Natalie. He wasn't sure how she'd react, seeing as how they hadn't had a significantly long relationship before the night of the play. But the one thing he knew was that he didn't want to go back to the way things were.

He was leaping, and he just hoped that the landing wouldn't hurt too much.

In the afternoon, he'd gone back over to the lodge, wanting to make sure everything was set up just how he wanted it to be. He'd had to move a few things, but with the lighting ready and the space open, he hoped tonight would be the beginning of the rest of their lives together.

He wasn't ready to propose by any means, as they still had a lot to work through. But he wanted her to see how sincere he was and to prove that he wasn't going to bail at the first—well, in this case, second—sign of danger.

"Shouldn't you be getting ready by now?" Walker asked, leaning against the door frame that led from the main lodge to the cultural hall.

"What time is it?" he asked before pulling out his phone from his pocket. The dance was set to begin at seven, and it was now six. He'd brought his suit in the truck on the chance that something like this happened. "Can I use your shower?"

"Which one?" his brother asked with a smirk. "I have several options here."

Easton strode toward him and then past him through the door. "Just the one you use will be fine." Tonight was going to be a big night. Part of him was ready for it, and the other part just wished he knew the outcome already.

He wasn't sure what time Natalie would show up, but he wasn't going to miss a moment at her side tonight.

CHAPTER 28

*B*y the time Lauren finished with her hair and makeup, Natalie couldn't stop staring at herself in the mirror. Lauren hadn't gone over the top on the makeup, for which Natalie was grateful, and she'd curled her hair and pulled it half-up, adding several small gems throughout the layers of hair.

They'd taken some time trying on dresses, some of them going in the no-go pile as soon as they hit her hips. In the end, she had to decide between a light blue ball gown and a bright red mermaid cut.

"What do you think?" Lauren asked her after she'd tried both on.

This was one of those decisions Natalie wished she could have asked someone else, either her grandmother or her own mother. But since neither was there, she turned to her father who'd been watching the scene on and off during football game commercials.

"Dad, which dress should I wear?" she asked, biting her lower lip. It felt a bit odd to ask him his opinion about something so opposite of sports, but considering how far they'd come in the past week, it felt right.

"Blue, definitely blue. You're my little princess. You might as well feel like one tonight." He winked at her, reminding her of all the times Easton had done so with that adorable dimple. As she thought of him, the butterflies took flight in her stomach.

She turned to Lauren. "Is Easton going to be there tonight?"

Lauren busied herself with putting all the makeup back in the bags and didn't meet her eyes. "I'm not completely sure. I didn't hear anything in particular about it, but I wouldn't be surprised if he dropped by to see how things were going." She stood and walked back over to the blue dress. "Let's get you dressed, Princess."

* * *

NATALIE LOOKED out the window to find the snow lightly falling against the darkening sky. How they'd spent so many hours getting ready, she wasn't quite sure, but it had all felt wonderful, from the manicure and pedicure all the way to having someone to chat with while curling hair and applying makeup. There were so many things she'd thought had gone from her life forever when her grandmother passed, but the number of people who'd appeared in support of her in the past few weeks was growing by the day.

Diane came over to the house just as Lauren was spraying her hair for the umpteenth time, and the surprised look on her face was everything Natalie could have hoped for. "You look breathtaking, Natalie. I hope you have a fantastic night!"

"I'm just a chaperone. This was just a fun afternoon, hanging out with a new friend." She squeezed Lauren's hand, grateful to have her there. They'd had enough time to talk about so many things that she felt like she knew the girl already.

"You never know what can happen. Maybe a little magic at the high school dance wouldn't be a bad thing." Diane grinned at her and walked over to greet her father. Even though they'd become close in the past few weeks, Natalie still couldn't watch them kiss and had to turn away to grab her coat.

Lauren disappeared into the room and came out wearing the red dress, her hair lightly curled behind her. "Are you ready for this?"

"As ready as I'm going to be. We should get going. I'm supposed to be there before the dance opens to start checking tickets." Natalie grabbed her keys and walked out the door, only to stop before walking out into the softly falling snow. How was she going to fit in her small compact car with this dress?

Lights turned on beyond her car, and Natalie did a double-take. Was that a limo? She turned to find Lauren at her side, buttoning her peacoat.

"Let's go!" Lauren said with excitement, pulling on Natalie's arm. They ran out, and the driver pulled open the back door, ushering them in.

Once they were all settled, Natalie frowned at the other girl. "What's really going on, Lauren? And how in the world do we have a limo in Coldwater Creek?"

The town was small enough that the thought of people actually using it regularly made her chuckle.

"I might be the one responsible for that. Since the lodge will be hosting things like weddings and other large events, I figured it would be a good investment to purchase a limo, with Walker's money, of course." She tipped her head to the side and laughed, causing Natalie to do the same.

"I've never been in one of these. It's actually really fun."

She glanced around the car as the driver pulled out, taking his time down the curving slopes.

Lauren gave her a wide-eyed expression. "You've never been in a limo? They're amazing! I think someone rented one from Alpine or Jackson back when I was in high school for prom. We thought we were so cool back then."

Natalie nodded like she understood what the other girl was saying. But the fact was, she hadn't been to any of the guys-ask dances during her high school years and had never had money to spring for a limo.

"Are you excited about the ball tonight? It will be a good way to refresh all those good memories of high school dances." Lauren wiggled her eyebrows.

Snorting, Natalie covered her nose and mouth with her hand for a few seconds until she'd gotten herself under control. "I never got asked to the fancy dances. I had a group of friends that would all go to the girls-ask ones, but those were less fancy."

"So, you've never actually been to a dance in a huge fancy dress and gotten to dance a slow song with the guy you like?"

Nothing like getting straight to the heart of things. "Nope."

Lauren's face split into a wide grin. "Then maybe this night will be better than you thought." She paused a second before asking, "Wait, didn't you dance with your husband at your wedding?"

It was one of those memories she had always tried to forget but somehow got brought up more than she cared to admit. "He was too drunk to dance and ended up puking during the part where we were supposed to cut the cake and do the first-dance stuff. I wish I had seen that as a sign at the time, but it's better that it's all in the past."

They chatted for the rest of the drive, and when they pulled up to the lodge, Natalie was blown away by the beauty of it. White lights had been hung along every eave of the lodge, and several lanterns filled with white light illuminated the path to the door.

"Wow! I can't believe they finished the lodge and got all this done."

"Designing is my favorite, so I might have added a few things to the to-do list," Lauren said, stepping out of the limo when the driver opened the door.

Natalie stepped out, grateful for the low heels Lauren had allowed her to wear instead of the sky-high ones. Chances of her making a fool of herself were slimmer if she was closer to the ground.

They walked into the large event room, and Natalie glanced around, taking in the beauty of the room. The tulle had been draped across the ceiling, as had several long ropes of white lights throughout. Small mounds of white were set up on either side of the stage, where a bunch of live band equipment was set up.

"I thought we were just going to have the usual DJ tonight. Did someone change that?" Natalie turned around, trying to find Lauren, who had disappeared.

Pulling her phone out of the small clutch, she saw it was six thirty, giving her plenty of time to check everything and then sit at the ticket booth to check the tickets as the students came in with their dates.

She walked over and hung her coat on a hanger of one of the large racks that had been brought in for the occasion. They should have put someone in charge of taking coats because this could end up being a mess later. She busied herself with other thoughts, causing her to jump when she heard a voice right behind her.

"Would you care to dance?" the familiar deep voice asked.

Turning around, she found herself only a few inches away

from Easton, the smell of his cologne wrapping around her like a blanket.

She tried to regain her composure as she took in the well-tailored suit and the baby-blue tie he'd worn. From there, she moved her gaze up to his face, the hint of that dimple peeking through.

"You clean up *well*," she said, her breath hitching as she realized how lame that sounded.

"And you look absolutely amazing. I have something for you." He walked over and pulled a small clear box from the floor next to the wall. How had she not seen it there? He moved in her direction, pulling a corsage that matched her dress from the box. Without saying anything, he slid it over her wrist, the touch of his fingers lighting her hand on fire.

Natalie chuckled. "What is that for? I'm just one of the chaperones for tonight. I don't need a corsage." Although her insides seemed to tell her otherwise. It was such a childish thing, to want to go to a nice dance all dolled up, and with the way Easton was looking at her, she didn't want to say no.

He reached out his hand, and she placed hers in it, feeling the warmth of his skin on hers. She smiled a bit at the callouses, knowing that only her Prince Charming could be so perfect and have something so real.

He led her out to the middle of the floor and started swaying. They'd gone a few steps when music started playing softly, and he pulled her closer to him, causing her breath to hitch again. All of the reactions she'd had the previous times they'd been together seemed to be heightened tonight, and she wondered if it was because this was the most romantic scene of them all, or just a fulfillment of one of her childhood dreams.

They moved in time to the music, and Natalie rested her head on his shoulder, feeling the most comfortable and safe she'd felt in quite some time. But the question was, why he was doing all this?

She lifted her head and looked into his dark eyes, trying to see what he was feeling in the dim light of the room. "Did you arrange all this?" She waved to the band and then her hair and dress.

"Parts of it. I definitely had some help from a few people."

"But why? Why go to all this trouble?" She bit her lip to keep from crying as tears sprang to her eyes unexpectedly.

He stepped closer, his gaze flicking from her eyes to her lips rapidly. "Because I wanted to ask for your forgiveness. There were a lot of things I messed up on, like not forgiving you as soon as you apologized and for taking so long to figure out how I felt about you. I was being selfish and protective, and I'm sorry. Will you forgive me for being an idiot?"

Natalie chuckled. "I think I can do that. But who told you about me wanting to dance?"

"Your father."

She stopped dancing, trying to keep from reeling. "My— my father told you about all this?"

"He just said you've never gotten to dance with someone while you were wearing a pretty dress. Lauren and Walker helped me put together the rest." He opened his mouth to say more but looked down first, as if trying to gather his thoughts. When he looked up, she saw the tenderness she'd grown to love about him.

"I also wanted to tell you, Natalie Hirsch Lynch, that I love you. I think I've loved you since I met you in your car, when you didn't want to listen to me as I—"

"I totally listened to you!" she cut him off.

He raised his hands and smiled, his dimple having the full effect on her. "You've always intrigued me, Natalie, and I was hoping you would be my girlfriend." He looked around the room and chuckled. "Does that sound too much like high school?"

Smiling wide enough to make her cheeks hurt, Natalie shook her head and moved closer, throwing her arms around his neck. "I would love to be your girlfriend." With that, she pressed her lips to his, finally taking in the warmth and the strength of them that she'd only dreamed of before.

He deepened the kiss, pulling her closer to him and making the inner debate between the need to breathe and the need to keep kissing him a reality. A cheer echoed through the room, and she pulled back just enough to see Lauren and Walker clapping from the doorway.

As she turned back to look at Easton, they were only an inch apart, and he leaned in and kissed her softly, causing everything inside her to want to jump up and down in excitement. She'd gone from feeling like her life was constantly falling apart to getting just about every wish fulfilled, all within a day.

Sure the changes hadn't all happened today, like the sudden liking Easton and her father had for one another, but she didn't want to dwell on the past any longer, grateful that she had a future worth working toward. She only hoped her grandmother was smiling as she was looking down on them from heaven.

The lights dimmed for the final scene of the spring play. Natalie couldn't believe how well the students had done, and once the curtains were drawn and the audience lights came on, she rushed back to congratulate each of them.

It seemed like the night kept extending as she stood in line, chatting with parents and other students who congratulated her on the success of the production. When the crowd died down and her students started heading home, she walked back out on stage one more time, wanting to relish the moment.

The last play had been soured by how things had gone with Easton, but it was amazing what had happened since then. She and Easton were doing better than ever, and she couldn't wait to see him when he got back in the morning from moving cattle.

She turned, ready to move off the stage and pack up for the night, when the spotlight turned on, causing her to raise her arm over her eyes to see into the seats. After a few tries of looking up to see who was manning the light, she gave up, knowing it was hopeless from this angle.

"Natalie." Easton's voice cut through the silence of the room, and she jumped back, not sure if she'd heard it in real life or just in her head.

"Easton? Where are you? What are you doing here?" She glanced around, trying to get her eyes to adjust so she could see into the shadows of the stage and down into the audience chairs.

He strode to the edge of the spotlight, a mischievous grin causing her to wonder what was happening. Though they'd been together almost four months, it seemed like his favorite thing was to surprise her with things, and she didn't quite mind it.

"We got done a bit early, and I wanted to see you." There was a slight tremor in his voice, and it looked like his hand was shaking a bit.

Natalie moved over to him, wrapping her arms tight around his neck and breathing in the outdoor scent that clung to him. She'd never thought she would love someone who liked both football and ranching, but those were a part of him, and she loved him for it.

She pressed her lips to his and pulled back, still curious as to why he was acting so strange. "Are you feeling okay?" Raising her right hand, she felt his forehead. Everything seemed normal.

"Actually, I wanted to talk to you about something." He paused, taking in a deep breath. "You know I love you, right?"

"Yes." She drew the "s" out, making the word sound longer than one syllable.

He pulled away from her and dropped down to one knee, having to stabilize himself with one arm so he didn't fall over.

Natalie's heartbeat pounded in her ears, and she clapped

her hands over her mouth in disbelief. This was definitely something she hadn't expected.

"I know we've only been dating a short while, but I'd prefer to make you my wife. Will you marry me?" He pulled out a small box with an intricate band and a solitaire cut diamond in the center.

"Of course I'll marry you," she said, kneeling down in front of him. She took his face with both hands and kissed him with all the promise in the world she could give him. "From football lights to stage lights, you're all I ever want."

* * *

Continue Ashley & Preston's story in *Love in a Snapshot*

* * *

Thank you for reading *Love Lights!* If you enjoyed it, I would love to see a review from you. You can also subscribe to Britney's newsletter here:
Subscribe to Britney's List

ALSO BY BRITNEY M. MILLS

Christmas at Coldwater Creek Series

Love in a Blizzard

Love in the Lights

Love in a Snapshot

Love in the Details

The Love, Austen Series

Love, Austen

Austen, Party of Two

Austen Unscripted

Matched, Austen

Austen, Edited

The International Billionaire Series

The Australian Billionaire

The French Billionaire

The British Billionaire

The Vegas Billionaire

The Italian Billionaire

Rosemont High Baseball Series

The Perfect Play

The Perfect Game

The Perfect Catch

The Perfect Steal

The Perfect Hit

Sage Creek Small Town Series

Loving His Flower Girl

Loving His Reporter Girl

* * *

Join Britney's newsletter

Get the latest updates on new releases and other fun tidbits!

ACKNOWLEDGMENTS

I'm so grateful to the team behind each of my novels. To my readers, my Advanced Reader team, thank you for taking the time out to help me find the little errors and make these books shine.

To my critique group: Bree Livingston, Deb Goodman, Shannon Symmonds, and Julie L. Spencer, thank you for your help and bits of wisdom to make these characters come to life.

To Christina Schrunk, my amazing editor, I'm so grateful for your ability to take the scraps of a story I have in my head and make it readable and enjoyable.

To Brenda for designing my amazing covers. Thank you for your patience as I figure out what each story needs to look like on the outside.

To Krista for proofreading and helping me catch all the little things.

To my husband and family for being the amazing support I need, especially around deadline time.

I can't wait to see what the next books bring!

Britney

ABOUT THE AUTHOR

Britney Mills was born in Utah but parts of her heart lie in Boston, Washington D.C. and Germany. Her love of writing began with the third grade book her teacher assigned her to write and she spent hours hidden behind her mother's couch writing pages and pages about knights and castles. Now she writes about romance. Go figure.

When she's not mothering her four small children, writing or reading, she's probably out playing a sport, going on a hike, or binge watching a murder mystery series. The way to her heart is through homemade chocolate chip cookies and five minutes peace.

www.ingramcontent.com/pod-product-compliance
Lightning Source LLC
Chambersburg PA
CBHW030757200726

48288CB00004B/1217